THE MAN FROM MAESFORD

Lesley Byard-Smith

UPFRONT PUBLISHING
LEICESTERSHIRE

THE MAN FROM MAESFORD
Copyright © Lesley Byard-Smith 2002

All Rights Reserved

No part of this book may be reproduced in any form
by photocopying or by any electronic or mechanical means,
including information storage or retrieval systems,
without permission in writing from both the copyright
owner and the publisher of this book.

ISBN 1 84426 139 5

First Published 2002 by
MINERVA PRESS

Second Edition 2002 by
UPFRONT PUBLISHING
Leicestershire

THE MAN FROM MAESFORD

HE HAD STARTED to talk to himself. 'I shall walk down this road,' he said, 'always.' This form of conversation had become a pleasure. He felt comfortable, the stones from the path hard on his feet.

Aledd Vaughan, the last of the Vaughans – Vaughan son of Vaughan – belonged here. He knew each twist in the road on his two-mile walk to work. A car shot by. He leaned hard against the hedge. Waved. Old man Marchell, mad. Slowly passing cattle and sheep, Aledd, at thirty-five was aware only of a good life stretching before him. He crossed onto a green road used by those on foot. He could walk like this for ever, his feet soft on soft turf.

No one had told him that things were changing; the half-built villa at the entrance to the village, fresh paint. Pulling fronds from the ferns, he walked on, racing the birds.

The town of Maesford looked down on a marsh, an empty place stretching to mountains. They called it the village that vanished. All that remained were some cottages, two or three joined together. Spreading north to a hill, the new settlement had formed a town. It eclipsed the older buildings below, leaving the church isolated in a field. Two families still bore local names. A handful of others with their relations, in the surrounding hill, kept close behind the walls of their farms, the windows like black eyes staring. Pronounced 'funny' by some, united in their culture, they trod old paths and did things in traditional ways.

No rules controlled their driving habits. The townsfolk cursed the lawless but the police seemed unaware of anything irregular. At the town end, a queue of cars would wait in the silence for friends to converse, and, as silently, a car might injure a man in a sunken lane, an event viewed as inevitable as the loss of a sheep or cow.

From this community Aledd made his way to the cottage shop. It stood wedged between a baker's and a general store in a makeshift sort of way, as a shelf might accommodate hardware. At times, when the streets were emptying, it only needed one person on the premises. It was possible to guess which entrance a customer would use – whether for bread, hard wear or a nick-nack for a birthday present – by the angle of a leg seen at knee height from a window overlooking a little track which rose steeply to join the main thoroughfare at right angles.

'Someone's coming!' The girl from the baker's tapped on the half-door.

'Me or you?'

Sometimes they swapped jobs and no one minded. Once a week the owner would walk through proprietarily with friends.

'I was determined not to change a thing!'

'You are lucky with your staff,' the friends would respond, and Sylvia Bailey would laugh and shake her head to suggest a happy accident, at the same time conveying it was no more than she deserved. The staff would look on in silence. Sylvia paid their wages.

Aledd's smile could fill a room. In the shop, as the door swung on its iron hinge and jerked the bell above, a warmth met the customer which seemed to extend to the objects on the shelves. He smiled. Someone was standing in the doorway. And as the colour in his face rose fast to the line of his eyes, he spoke, and the voice had warmth. They were drawn in.

'How nice to see you.' Now the smile. People went away feeling better.

It was most agreeable when the owner was away. He ignored the catalogue of extra duties. He would rearrange things and manage to add to the takings. Everyone approved. At first small changes were made, cakes among the antiques, candles in corners. 'You might move that bloody bell,' someone suggested.

Aledd replied with a smile.

He put a board in the road with an arrow. Flower baskets and chairs appeared on the pavement. 'Teas', in a fancy hand, on the door which had changed colour, and he took to wearing a red apron.

One morning with a screech of tyres, Sylvia Bailey got out of her black Mercedes. The open roof had made her flushed or she had sensed there was something wrong. No one crossed her. She snatched up the TEA sign, threw it down and flung open the door. The bell died before she spoke. Aledd stood, a table held to his chest on his way out.

'What...' Sylvia's cry choked more words. 'What...?' With tears in her eyes she elbowed her way through, the table grazed his face. She called out, 'Lynne, are you there?'

The girl stayed in the shadows.

Aledd tried to speak but the woman was at him again. Words flew past his ears like a flock of birds. She was pulling cloths off tables. A spoon fell on the floor. A customer slipped away unnoticed. Looking up she found a bird in a cage.

'Get out!' she screamed. 'Both of you are fired!'

He looked like a man sleepwalking after his dismissal. The hours that before had danced by, were slow and gave no shape to the day. He spent some time at his mother's. Then on a tide of local sympathy, he was given a job at a cafe and, soon, a job in a bar. The colour returned to his face as he leaned over the pumps and glasses.

'Prices down for a full house!' He made jokes.

He had never been so popular. He dreamed of his own pub. His former assistant, Lynne, now his regular girlfriend, was enjoying domesticity in a cottage he had been lent. Like many hill dwellings it nestled between mountains as a protection against extremes of weather. Farms survived with this design, but light and warmth was experienced for only a few months of the year and, in a bad summer, the sun was rarely seen to dry out the perpetual dampness. The two were young and, to begin with, they hardly noticed it. At one time the view might be shut out by cloud and at another it appeared as pretty as a postcard. Each day he would arrive with another piece of furniture and she would find rags of blanket or curtains to transform the place, running to greet him when he returned in borrowed transport. Together they giggled and ate rabbit and drank warm beer. In a few weeks there was a garden for vegetables and a flower patch. Some beans survived, with encouragement, but the flowers died.

Lynne caught a cold that wouldn't go. She accepted it as part of the price they must pay for happiness until she began to feel ill. At night, before they extinguished the lamps, he would wrap her in a blanket when she started to shiver, usually after their supper of stew. He dosed her with whisky and sugar and rocked her to sleep.

He worked a day shift but one night he was late. Eager to tend his patient with spoils from various friends, he stopped and stared into the darkness. The house had gone. He was in the wrong place. He peered into the night until the outline of stone emerged. He found his way to the door. It was open. He called, his voice faded. A rank odour he had never noticed before, cooking oil and the sickly smell of dirt and crumbling cement, repelled him.

'Lynne,' he called again. 'Lynne.' Inside there was nothing but raw air. Events had overtaken him. In working long hours he had neglected her. The darkness was impenetrable. Shining the van lights through the cracked glass of the kitchen area, he found matches and a candle. He lit another and a lamp before he noticed the letter.

Lashing trees and leaves in the lane, he drove the van to her parents' door. He thought of nothing but her welfare. For a second time he experienced a flood of accusations before he could plead his case. It was hard for him to believe his concern was unrecognised. Stoically he bore the abuse. He had come as a friend. Lynne's father, pound for pound, was his size, his eyes hooded, level with his own, his cheeks dark mottled. With every word the pores of his skin seemed to produce pinpoints of hate that opened and ran with sweat down the side of his nose. Aledd had ceased to listen to the words. It seemed safer to hold his ground, feet rooted, legs braced until the man hit him. He waited for the blow that never came, walked shakily from the house, got in the van and drove away, his vision blurred. He said nothing to his mother and she was not a woman to ask.

After work the next day he was forced to return to the cottage to collect some things. He approached with emotion. The building like a pet dog waited. Now he would go back home.

Work reassured him and he received praise. Aware of whispers, he took no notice, to be popular was to be talked about.

Sylvia Bailey started her campaign from the moment her shop was, she said, 'Desecrated.' Losing a picture during the shop's continuous reshuffle, 'He was a menace.' She gave the words peculiar emphasis and kept his bicycle with the wages he was too nervous to ask for. He was a 'warlock', kidnapping a girl and taking her up in the hills. The police were alerted. Each day he immersed himself in work, each night he planned the return of his committed partner, writing a journal for company. To his friends he said nothing.

Just as life was resuming a comfortable rhythm, he was shocked by a letter. There had been others sent and received on his behalf and forgotten, but this was like a knife and he was wounded.

'Now is the time.' His friends wanted action.

'You must,' they said. But events had disabled him.

Politics was not his world and the law was television. So he let them do it, whatever it was, or do it to him, not caring much about money. He seemed the same in public but his colour had gone. Sometimes a film of sweat appeared on his face that might have been grease or heat from the kitchen. He began to dread the postman and the telephone made him jump. Embarrassed, he made a joke of it. Days went by and he settled again to a way of life that suited him, starting early and in slow motion prepare for the steady flow of people. He rarely had a drink but smoked a lot, escaping to a back shed in the pub's new garden. It was a recently designed hostelry, in a prime position for business but from this new world he must continuously retreat. To feel in place a cool round cigarette, to strike a match and with the first intake of smoke, forget uncertainties, remember he was once another person, this was a holiday. He could take this other person back with him into the bar, smiling the old smile for an easy exchange of words.

Sun shone through the open window, lit the curtains edge, caught the gloss of paint, the glass and beer pumps. It made him pick up a cloth, polish in more light, stop and talk again. Later he went for walks, always the same way. He trudged familiar paths, noted the formation of ruts that changed each season, growth of grass that fell under the rain or bent by the sun and crushed by cattle. Out on the hill he strode swinging his legs, the wind in his face. Once he met Lynne. She thought he was seeing someone else.

A policeman was standing by the farm gate. He nodded, smiled and pushed past unsuspecting. Inside his mother was mopping tea stains from the plastic tablecloth. She did not look up. There was someone behind him. He spun round and fear for the first time stopped him. He froze. No thoughts came. He saw his mother pale in the half vision from the corner of his eye, her hands red round the ball of cloth wiping tea stains like spots of blood among the faded flower patterns. She dabbed the cloth in time with his heartbeat.

'I don't want you to worry. I'm just doing my job. Routine. We have a complaint and I must investigate.' Aledd remembered he was at school with this man.

'They're giving me a terrible time.' The man was sitting at the wiped table now.

'I'll get tea.' His mother's voice was a breath.

'No, no. Not for me.'

'Let her.' Aledd now felt in control.

'Okay, Mrs Vaughan. It's bad for us all... I've been through the house and the barns.' He stood again to address Aledd. 'Where were you on 3 July?'

Aledd could not remember. He thought of his journal started a few weeks later and determined to continue with it. It gave his life a purpose.

'More news about that awful man!' Sylvia Bailey interrupted her husband's progress from office to car. A habit he hated and contrived to avoid as it disturbed the placid flow of his thoughts. He stopped and looked down as if in search of firm ground.

'The Jeromes are back.'

The Jeromes were Sylvia's special friends, 'like her'. She let it be known, and known as many ways possible to the Jeromes themselves, hoping they would reciprocate. She looked for signs of success. She had a host of friends and acquaintances who were never quite right, quite 'like her' or, of course, the Jeromes. Not expecting her husband's reply, the news was not withheld.

'He's a bad lot. I knew there was something. They'll tell you at dinner.' The Jeromes, whose presence in the newer town was an advantage, had for generations been the head of the old village, lent style. Sylvia hoped it would rub off. She dared not dwell much on her own shortcomings in case she saw, as others might, that they precluded her from other friends. In the Jeromes continual absences, she lacked backing. They were often abroad in some metropolis or deserted coastal region too select for comment.

Today's little success came after a chance meeting when she spoke, generating concern about her trouble. She was led away to coffee extending to lunch, during which she learnt the history of the Maesford man. Always one to give as well as she got, she elaborated on a version of strange happenings in the mountains that left her friends bewildered and not a little shocked.

'Very sad, very sad,' they murmured, 'a foolish young man.' To them he was still young at thirty or forty. At their age, the decades blurred.

'It seems wherever he went, there was trouble,' Sylvia explained. Particulars of troubles, assorted and inconclusive as the troubles themselves, sounded unsatisfactory now.

'Enough to say there have been incidents,' Sylvia concluded.

'Death?' interrupted her husband. 'Nothing so shocking?'

'Shut up, Edward,' Sylvia snapped and went on where she had left off.

Every few days she would turn up in his den like the queen of spades. His hand froze in air between desk and drawer.

'Things used to go missing here, now I remember.'

'What?'

'Loo rolls.' She would vanish again until an hour later.

'The Jeromes would lose garden tools. Just before they left for somewhere. I forget where it was.'

'Loo rolls. Garden tools.' Edward's voice held no question.

'It was soon after our experience that they chose to tell me. They have known him since he was a child, and the whole family.

11

Thinking back, as we are all thinking back, there is something very irregular, a history of something sinister, I won't say wicked – the Jeromes won't say "wicked" but others will,' she ended in a whisper. 'Thinking back, you see, that explains it. These people from interbreeding are strange. Witches and warlocks come from such close communities. You're always reading about it.'

'Am I?'

'Fortunately there are few of them left!'

'Just one.' Edward used his flat voice.

'I'll let you know if we think of anything else.'

There was silence again and a wafting air after the door closed. The summer was exceptional.

Living each in their family home, the village pair were sometimes seen to escape to the mountains. It had been necessary after their hurried departure for some one to keep an eye on the cottage and make use of the little gifts of food and small luxuries that were often left on the back step as was customary in special cases. As her health improved Lynne was expected to fend for herself and, in such a large household as hers, she could absent herself without comment to the point where she could leave permanently again, unnoticed. Her mother, who once demurred, now turned away to deal with noisier problems.

Aledd and Lynne were together and the sun shone for that quarter of the year. He was pleased to see her redecorate the place after his amateur carpentry. Domestic chores seem to revive her and she looked happy. Plants, after a freezing spring, took well in boxes and flowered, rainbow coloured. These were Aledd's hours of peace and if a day was disturbing this was sanctuary. Over the third hill, a pool, in a place where as children they had played, held for him a fascination and excitement in its mirrored depths. Warned that it was a bottomless pit – as mothers controlled adventurous children – he long ago discovered it produced a kind of glow or healing power, or so he imagined, when on certain hot days he bathed there. In sultry weather the water would evaporate to expose a mossy basin, and breaking the reflection of clouds and sky, he would fall into ice from heat at the end of the day and, experiencing a sudden rush of energy, he would rise from the water, shining among the reeds while the wild horses looked on or moved idly away.

Today they walked together at first, but soon he was ahead.

'Come on up, it's magic,' he said, the girl waiting on a level below. 'Why won't you?'

'No, I hate it.'

'Rubbish.'

'Anyway it's cold. It's always cold.'

'No it's hot.'

The shallow edges, heated gently by the sun, tempted him, but he couldn't persuade her in. Sometimes at the cottage, she would sulk if she knew he was restless and determined to wander off. This time she pleaded with him to stay. He laughed at her. He set off at a run until breathless he slowed to a stop. Lynne, who had followed at a distance, losing sight of him, stood and looked around. She could hear nothing but sheep cropping the turf. She felt isolated on the empty mountain with only the hollow rhythmic sound of grazing sheep.

Sylvia took her dog by manicured lawns through lanes of mixed hedges to an open space with a view, but in her present state it was an unsatisfactory exercise.

'That person gets on my nerves,' was her excuse when she set off on a new and planned excursion. Similar comments used as excuses for any break in routine aroused her husband's interest.

'I'm beginning to think you fancy him, as the children say.'

'I won't dignify that with an answer.' She swept out. Her fury made him chuckle as one who has found a mouse to tease a cat. It became a game with him and always drove her from the house which had become her hermitage after the shop's closure.

She took the dog in the car, was off down the lane to the town and shops, on to her abandoned business premises, skirting the old village to a gap in the mountains. Three hills, round as basins drawn in a child's picture, were ahead of her. Beyond them, layer upon layer, mountains named after their colours, red and black, different in season, blue in the distance, misty where the clouds were low. She parked. Walking with the dog on a lead as bidden among the multitude of sheep, she was surprised to see a human form, but amidst the scrubby gorse and heather was a picnic group. It was not what she had expected and, a little disappointed, she trudged on until there were no cars left and the roads bare. She turned off to where she knew worn tracks must lead to some place of interest. Impatient to be let off the lead the dog jerked and howled. It was not pleasant but proved a diversion that exorcised the unease she had felt for the last half hour. The path dipped, the dog scraped unsteadily along cuts made by a tractor. Her feet slid in her damp shoes. Unused to rough ground she had not thought to provide herself with boots or country footwear. Before her was a belt of water run through with tyre treads and the marks of cattle. Mud trailed in an upward direction. Surely this was not the only point of interest in this desert.

Her feet hurt but she went on and as the ground rose, a clump of bracken on one side tempted her to lie back on the soft green fronds. She let the dog free. He lay also gratefully panting as a cloud came over the sun. The temperature had changed from hot to cold. She rose to go. There was nothing here. The dog leapt among the shoulder high thick green growth. She had to make a choice. No sane person would wander alone and shoeless along unvarying paths, although she might regale dinner guests with a tale of adventure. She must return. As the cloud passed, the earth warmed again. She put a blistered foot on the pads of moss and more daringly in the creaming mud. There was no one to see. How safe and soothing it was. How doubly shocking to see ahead of her a girl with dark hair. She was being watched. A path, twisting to a higher level, rose to a hill only now in view. Her foot lost contact with her shoe. She looked down briefly. It was no more than a second. When she looked back the girl had gone. As a woman of decision her mind made up, she walked, stumbled, away back through the cart ruts, slowly descending, putting as much distance between herself and what she later referred to as her distressing experience.

The girl, crouched in the heather, gave way to misery. She bent her head down to where the coarse fibres of shrub grazed her skin and tried to cry. A noise in her throat, strange and unbidden, brought no tears, forced its way into her neck and ears. Her head was bursting. Her eyes became knots of flesh that burned. She raised her head for an instant, fell forward into the heath choking.

A sound in so remote a place brought him from the water. He listened. It came again. He ran, wet as a fish to a terraced ridge and saw her. 'Lynny,' he called, and again as he flung himself across the wasteland of scrub to where she lay. He lifted her and placed her a few feet above him on a bank. His feet were bleeding. 'Lynny,' he kept repeating and lifted her again. She opened her eyes and closed them. They lay by the pool, the water cool in the shallows, the sun of fire.

'You were with that woman. Let me die.'

'There's no woman, Lynny, you were dreaming.'

'The Bailey woman.'

'Where?'

'Down there.'

'Where?'

'Or was it here, in this evil place.' She flung herself forward with both arms in the water. The glass pool smashed and the reflection of clouds collapsed in the dark water where her face had been, escaped over her head, her hair floating.

'Don't.' He was pulling her gently back, but kneeling she jerked free, forcing her head below the surface again, her wet clothes winding around her. The image was so horrifying he forgot the cold and fell towards her, arms and legs grappled and bound themselves to her in the reeds. He kicked to the bottom and felt stones. She floated, her face towards him. As he kissed her, her mouth was hot under the cold skin. The sun burned the cloud away and bore into his back. He dragged at her clothes as she floated, and unconscious of either heat or cold, only an impulse to let her take him down with her. He saw the water ripple in her smile. He stood and pulled her onto him, she floated away and he pulled her forward again. Legs round her waist like a drifting log he pulled her back to life.

On the bank, the sun shone.

'I think I'm pregnant.'

'I don't think so,' he said.

Wrapped in shirts and towel, in sodden shoes they didn't speak. The water had brought them together. He held her so she was weightless over the ground.

The incident of the 'Bailey Woman' gave him a secret sense of power. He took to driving his van past Hill House when he thought she might be there. He did not believe she had been looking for him, but she did have a dog to walk. Up the hill, through the town, the road was little used at the residential end, convincing him that his presence would be noticed as the labouring engine shuddered past each drive. He looked straight ahead, his eyes fixed on the tarmac. If she saw him he would be unaware. After this game of his, he would return down the back lanes and skirt the hill to the low lands.

For Lynne, the Bailey woman was not a joke. After a night of tender words she was uncommunicative. He feared she might succumb again to sickness after the scene at the mountain pool. 'Mawn Pools', as they were known, appeared where the peat was densest, sinking under the weight of accumulating water. Used by sheep and cattle, the largest and highest pool seemed to have an attraction. For him it was renewal, for her a force of something darker. It would be a long time before he persuaded her there again. At the cottage he tried to comfort her with blankets and alcohol. But she sat tense, said the place stank. She spent more time with her parents after that, and when he dropped her off in the town for shopping, he never knew if she would return to him.

When they were told to leave the cottage, Lynne cried all night in his arms. When he made love to her she cried more. As the first birds woke she slept, her face wet on his chest. He could not sleep. He listened to the birds as they stirred in the dim light as if they had a message for him. In despair he tried to make up words to their songs to pass the time until dawn. The dawn was full of sunrays. He moved and Lynne opened her eyes and smiled until the shock came back as she remembered their life had changed.

It was a relief to go to work even when people told him he looked tired. The pub was a success; the cottage was never theirs anyway. They could still be together, he said, and wondered if she believed him. Her family, he knew, were unhappy about their daughter's lifestyle. He gave her all the money he had for clothes for the weekend when he would take her out. The breakdown of their close association began to worry him but he still had faith that help would come as it had before. Loss could equal gain.

Once more criticism put him centre stage. It appealed to his sense of drama. He answered questions as one used to interviews and went to live at home.

He was aware a storm was gathering. The inhabitants of the hill town gossiped at home and spoke publicly of mysteries that soon became crimes. Lynne was crying at night again, she told him.

That he loved her was not in question, but to witness the emotional struggle that had become her daily torment was taking its toll. If they parted, life would be easier.

He experienced relief as he closed the door of the cottage for the last time. He had been told firmly and finally to give back the key he always left in the broken door. He took Lynne back to her parents' gate and strode off in the direction of the old farm. He could empty his mind of personal cares in the wind that blew in his face, the mist that came up from the valley and took out the rain. His strength returned and the firmness of his step. He felt young again. Now he was running. He stopped to lean over a fence, and anxiety that made him weary before, wrapped around him like a blanket. He tore himself away and went on down a slope and felt free again. He knew he must stay that way. He would see Lynne. The recollection made him miserable. He must work.

He arrived at the pub refreshed. Everyone was pleased with this transformation. He was himself again and his little laugh returned, lost the next day when Lynne cried, found in the sunshine and the open air. He was to see her, red eyed, drinking tea with his mother.

Pity and pain combined to strengthen his resolve, and with new purpose he shrugged off the fear of any retribution and determined to live for the moment. He went for his usual walk. Light from behind a cloud streamed across the valley. He took it as a sign. At work he thought of nothing but the task before him, took on more until days and nights seemed one.

The seasons were changing and with them a change of mood. He still found relief in the air of the hills but the mists came in a curtain and the wild horses the colour of ashes looked questioningly at him through their dark manes. The bracken, cut and baled for bedding left a bleak world of bare land and shadow.

There were changes, the customary migrations from place to place, houses changing hands, a popularity swap. Only an insider would know what word or deed would mark a man and lose him business. More remarkable still, the state could change; go into reverse without his knowledge.

The Bailey's garden redesigned, glowed with flowers. The guest wing extended to a swimming pool. Walled to replicate a Greek bath, the whole was intended to contain the Bailey's daughter, a quiet girl with mood swings. As was customary with college students, Elida was having a year off before studies, which grew to two years after a course change and her determination to live near the sea.

'You'll have a long way to go,' sighed her mother.

'Driving lessons,' advised her father before they compromised with a pool.

'It was to do with my name,' she told her parents.

'Blame your mother. She's the one who likes Ibsen,' her father concluded and afterwards called her Lizzie.

Her mother, embarrassed by her lack of parental bond, resorted to apology when friends enquired after her, her absence palpable through the echoing house. But the resourceful Sylvia soon turned it to advantage, inventing prospects of national or international success in a career unspecified, there being little chance of her deception uncovered. Her daughter's infrequent homecomings would need explanation but Elida would not explode the myth. Her long silences were notorious. Without a boyfriend or another girl, she could sit at the table without opening her mouth except to feed it, and circulate during the rest of the day without a sound beyond an irritating hum.

'We must conclude,' Edward said, 'she's composing.'

For her next visit she arrived at night by taxi. She ate smoked salmon sandwiches with her parents looking on, drank a bottle of wine with her parents helping out, slept, rose as usual and was next observed talking to the new gardener, a not so young but chatty man. Sylvia feared what he was telling her.

'Come on darling, we're doing your shopping, remember?'

Wearing her 'Lizzie' look Elida obediently came as bidden, with a wave to the gardener.

'What happened to the other one?' she asked, getting reluctantly into the car.

'Come on lazy bones,' her mother purred, 'don't you want a surprise?'

Lizzie became 'Elida' and sighed.

'A car?'

'Ooh, Mummy!'

Sylvia had battles, but she had weapons.

Why did he feel threatened? Why was his heart cold? Tiredness could make a child of a man. When he was small he was set upon by bigger boys. Taken by surprise he could never fight and cried when he got home to his mother. Today he remembered as he passed that particular spot and experienced loss like bereavement. He was missing Lynne. He jumped in the van and drove to the town. He looked for her in the street. Groups of people gave him back confidence. He went on a mile up to Hill House where he saw, not turning head but out of the corner of his eye, two women standing in the garden and his confidence slipped away. Sylvia Bailey threatened him, her presence, even her name. Standing there with a friend he supposed, he felt outnumbered. Leaving Hill House behind he went on for a time, down small lanes, circling the plain, the foothills and the farm. A plan, half formed, had taken shape and spread before him like a new country. He drove on, though the light was failing, past the farm. There were places on his home ground he could find without a lamp. He stopped. The dark grew around him but, as he looked up, the sky still shimmered with a far light. Below his line of vision the trees and boulders stood in silhouettes, dark against dark, with a nimbus glow. He looked down into blackness but knew where to go. He reached a plateau and felt the ground. He was on the edge of a plantation. The bare space ploughed long ago still retained a fringe of vegetation. He trailed his fingers through the tender plants, began plucking the feathery growth stuffing it into his shirt. He recovered the van. In the excitement at having found what he was looking for he had lost the path, the road, and any sense of time. He was alone. The owls broke the silence but he did not wish to be caught. He was in the van. He was riding like a highwayman. He lowered the windows and felt the rush of air, heard the tyres race. Later, hiding his treasure in a shed, he slept without food or drink content with his new freedom. For days he hugged his secret, a close and special friend, slipping away to spread and dry his plants in a place he hoped no one would find.

Like an automaton he went to work in the empty bar. At length, people came in, in ones and twos. They seemed remote from him. To the big houses on the hill they looked with something like the old deference. Life had returned to familiar ways but with an exclusion zone around his pub, The Bell. Bothered by people who gave advice his warmth turned to acerbity. 'Go home,' he would say. 'Go home. This is The Bell and I'm going to ring it.' And there was no humour in his voice. They had been wrong about him, they grumbled. Boy turns to man and hardens. They left, and in the way of things, came back again. Just a trickle at first and then a stream. They had registered disapproval.

A letter arrived. It was a long brown envelope like a bill. It was typed. After reading it he went back again, studied the typeface, the address. Comprehending little he opened the innocent thing. Evil would surely bear a mark or shadow to indicate poison or prepare him for a shock. He had opened it at last without thinking more of it, perhaps a bill he would settle or save to settle. His hand was shaking as he started to read.

'Go back to your village you are not wanted here.'

He always experienced a pounding of his heart, attending to the mail. So many shocks. The pounding continued through the day.

The first customers were farmers, friends of the family, old and sane. He would speak to them; they presented friendly faces, strong as rocks. He stood before them on trial.

'What's the matter, boy?'

He thought first they had seen his fear, second, they were criticising slow service. He pulled some beer, waiting for the stream of liquid to thrust up the cream froth slowly, and slowly, after he had placed the black drink before them, he held out the paper, shadowed he imagined with hate.

'It's hate mail – hate mail.'

'Hate mail?'

'Hate mail!'

'Hate mail.' They wouldn't stop.

'I don't understand,' Aledd began.

'It's about that girl of yours.'

'Her father, George!'

''E'd never!'

'No, never! Take it to the police.'

The police read it. He had waited four days, during which he suffered mixed emotions. He thought of Lynne. 'I love you,' he told her on the phone, asking to see her but not disclosing his purpose.

'I love you, too,' she said, 'but I'm going out, do you mind?'

'Going out where?'

'With someone.'

'Who?'

'I don't know. I mean if somebody asks me.'

He made no answer.

'It's that damn pool, you know. Best keep away.'

There was something unusual about the pool, it might help him in his trial. That evening he went to the third mountain. 'Don't go there, people say, and I go,' he said to himself, and, aloud, 'here I am,' shouting to the wind. He faced into the roar of air, the wind was always highest at this point. The sensation made him laugh and he went home.

Suddenly everyone knew about it, everyone was talking. In the village sympathy, from the hill town, threats.

'He nearly killed that Marchell girl – you know – Lynne Marchell, Lynne... About at night, black rites, blood on the heather, clothing... drugs, I wouldn't wonder.'

Aledd had not returned to his cache of weeds in the old shack. Ruined and forgotten on the furthest cleft of the hills, it belonged to no one and, according to rule, a person could stake his claim if it was for legitimate use. More ideas were growing in his head and his hands ached to make them reality. He would build a house.

'Look mate,' the policeman said, 'get rid of it, you know what I mean?' Aledd didn't answer.

'We are on your side.'

Aledd gave him his half smile.

'You know what I mean,' the policeman went on. 'Get rid of the stuff, okay?'

Could a man read his thoughts? He waited until after dark. Who had seen? The eyes of the stones? A shepherd? He wondered now if the steady stare of Mel Price was saying more than thanks for his steak and chips every day. Seasonal cuts for regulars.

On a night of mist he went with a torch and found his dried leaves safe as a nest where he had left them. He gathered them wrapped in paper, a bulge in his pocket with a rabbit he had acquired. Then he left for home, not wanting to plan to rebuild his hideaway until his nerves had settled. He became the hunter hunted, racing home, thinking only where he could hide his treasure.

'Come home, Elida,' Sylvia Bailey ordered.

Home to Elida was a country at war. Her spirits sank each time she spoke the word. It troubled her more for its store of parental stress than for any unpleasantness or poor architecture. When there, she must perform.

'We all do!' her father assured her, and continued to describe a world stage, which fact gave little comfort and provoked another wave of misery. She had a photograph of the swimming pool complex designed for her privacy, but she knew her mother would check her hours of freedom against some duty, however small, that loomed like a cloud to darken her day. She would watch the hand of the clock as it crept around. Each five minutes drawing her nearer to a social function, where her mother held court. The more a theme developed the more her eyes sought her feet, sweeping the floor in search of comfort. It was a trick of her father's Sylvia noted, but was never sure whether it was copied or involuntary.

This dread of cocktail hours, or tea or coffee, carried over into more weighty moments of the year. Christmas, birthdays, holidays – bank or summer – elections, job interviews, the year seemed packed with obstacles to be faced and overcome. Life had become a nightmare. In vain did her father and at least one acquaintance point out her eligibility. She was aware she was nice but not pretty and not very clever. Money was available but brought no peace. Her favourite occupations were walking and swimming and lounging around with a book. The last provoked most comment but it was pleasant in the sun, in a hammock, or the long grass under the apple trees and it was awkward to explain she didn't really want to do anything. It should be possible to find someone to do nothing with. She had tried bringing friends back but knew they expected more than her great silences and rural exhibitions. Failing with two boys she might try a girl she supposed, then her mind closed at this point. She thought about local attractions. There was one, be it a last resort, and she chanced it.

'I can pay,' she said to a girl she had met recently, 'you don't need money.' And it worked. Failure threatened when the friend declared she could only manage a week and that in the middle stage of the summer break.

'Any men?' It was a question she was ready for. She had an imaginary list of handsome admirers. Some had substance, existing on farms, in shops or service areas, real enough to smile on when she dared, and, trembling, to be smiled on back. She packed and went home, to phone her friend each evening. It was a great stroke of luck not only to find a new gardener – and talkative – but to glimpse another man, altogether more than usually fetching, Aledd, in a new sprayed van. She was pretty certain he had seen her but chose to look the other way.

'Elida!' Sylvia had started her assault.

Elida's optimism failed. Life was hell as usual.

'Elida, I hope you are not going to spend the holiday talking to the gardener.' Elida looked down with her pendulum eyes.

'I don't want you to be a snob but you must find more suitable companions.'

'Where?' Her despair had surfaced again.

'If you don't know I'll find some for you.'

Life was once again to be circumscribed by her mother.

It only took a word to change for ever her view of the future. The conversation at dinner turned to 'the man', known generally in their circle as 'The Man From Maesford', making the moment bright with the possibility of future contact with him. Elida was communicating, her mother thanked goodness.

'There's nothing like a good gossip,' the Jeromes admitted. 'But we do hope – John and I have talked – that there will be no witch-hunt coming from this. There may be a court case we know.' As no one knew who was to be summoning whom, they all laughed, especially Elida.

'I have an idea so amazing you won't believe,' she told her friend. 'It is so daring you may not want to do it. I certainly can't tell you on the phone.'

Her friend was hooked and, in high excitement, Elida wrote her a letter. Enthusiasm bore her down the town the next day to appear in Aledd's bar.

Luckily it was empty except for the local shepherd in a corner. Aledd didn't recognise her at first when she bought some cider. Sitting in the window watching him, he knew, as he glanced up at last from the assembly of glasses, that he had seen her before somewhere. He flushed as he thought of Sylvia Bailey, but treated her daughter to a smile. She said nothing, drank her drink and seemed to be writing a letter. She looked straight at him as she left as if inclined to speak but had not formulated a sentence. She stopped at the door and again made an effort to say something. Until this moment no one had noticed her. The shepherd seemed to be counting sheep.

Summoning courage, 'How are you?' she said and averted her eyes.

'Fine,' he said.

Sylvia Bailey was so surprised that her daughter had indulged in any activity other than sitting by the swimming pool or lying in bed, she didn't ask questions. Her father was concerned. His anxiety took from him the comments he habitually made. He said nothing. Elida had had a good day.

At dawn she was up and after breakfast examined her new car.

'Don't drink and drive!' Her mother would never release her without a dusting of words.

'I'm only going for a drive,' and then added, remembering her old fancy, 'to look for water!'

'Well, you won't find any here,' Sylvia said darkly.

Aledd, his character under scrutiny, was determined to be unmoved when faced with distortions of the truth or outright lies. He had confronted the enemy. The Bailey daughter had acknowledged him with a murmur and a nod. A group of smart looking people in the street had returned his smile. It relieved the pressure. He was pleased with these little incidents which proved a point and raised his self-esteem. He felt satisfied when speaking to a solicitor that he was well supported and these daily conversations replaced entries that once filled his journal.

'Go for it!' urged the little team in the bar. 'Defamation of character!' they bayed. They were on his side.

He was supposed to ask for damages, but as time went on, the idea seemed more and more preposterous. Fearing further humiliation, he was content with a letter of complaint to salvage his reputation. 'Forget it now,' he said and lived two lives.

During the day he cooked at The Bell. Results varied. At night he started to build a house. He took to sleeping in his barn, four walls, a bit of roof and a chimney. With only a rag bed, it was worse than the cottage and the shepherd's hut on the hill below, but the van, kept polished, showed his will to succeed. He dragged up old timbers and pinched new wood, found slates and slabs of stone, and with his small earnings bought roofing felt. Corrugated iron, rusting red, stained his hands and clothes. He came down from the hills a red man, washing as best he could at the pub. But as his appearance deteriorated, he became a source of jokes. A 'Rusty Nail', the latest cocktail, was continually ordered with sniggers. The workload was punishing. He took to rising earlier and losing hours of sleep. He was aware he was tired through little omissions. He would misjudge the time or fail to lock a door. He lost interest in the job, more important now to finance the materials he had invested in. He was disinterested in food. The daily recipes were replaced by an assembled chaos of vegetables. He ate little or nothing. His once deft hands no longer obeyed him but clumsily groped their way to closing time, a pile of empty pots and glasses confronting him when his head was full of saws and nails. It took a great effort of will to run hot water and complete cleaning tasks.

Heat and soap bubbles began to restore life to his fingers. He pressed his hands down in the water and watched the lather rise above his wrists turning them pink. He thought of warm baths as the bubbles spread like a soft bed and the steam, a drug. But the demons that would not let him rest drove him out of the door to another world that was waiting.

The afternoon was still warm before evening brought the chill of a new season.

Studying his accumulation of materials, slate and stones and substantial pieces of rock, he felt with excitement an artist's pride. He started work again, building. The light would slowly fade. He noticed the mist laying down moisture over cold surfaces, on the roof he felt dizzy and climbed down. He sat on some bricks and measured small wood, laying the pieces beside him. He worked longer than he intended, aware of sheep as he leaned against the wall. Sharp corners of stone dug in his back, but grateful that his legs could rest he laid his hands palm upwards on his lap. They felt heavy as the bricks. He placed them by his side, they became detached from his body, his legs were tree trunks, and his arms were logs.

His head felt cleared now, his back was numbed from pressure that let him float to another country. Plastic flapping on the roof became sails of a ship. The breeze had brought cloud and the light was fading. He looked at the watch bought with his first wages. He was hours late.

He arrived to find someone had opened a side door to let in the regulars who all seemed to be drinking. NOT PAID said a list on the bar. There was always someone who knew where the window was open or the hidden place of a spare key.

'You look bad,' said the know-all, and he was given whisky and felt better and ate half a sandwich. The rest of the day seemed to disappear.

It had started to rain as he drove into the hills. It was pouring by the time he took the mountain pass and reached his new home. The tarpaulin had come off the roof from the most secure struts. He tied rope and working with ladder and old corrugated iron, forgot his spinning head. He'd finish what he had started, work through the night if he must, then rest and sleep. He was aware he was cold as he pulled off his sodden clothes, found a jacket and wrapped himself in a damp blanket. A kettle and stove, mug and hot-water bottle, a memory of Lynne, were near him, but he was too weary to move from his grey cocoon. Water dripped down the wall at his side. He longed for the whisky he had secreted and forgotten to bring. He remembered his mother's stockpot full of meat pieces, Lynne to laugh as she did when they met that first year. The primus stove and instant coffee were four feet away but he felt his strength leaving like some member of the family he thought would remain for ever but was departing, walking slowly away. He jerked awake, turned over, reached out, shifted his position and lit a lamp. The effort made him shudder. He tried to remember his dream but it was morning now, warmer yet colder. His feet were cold and his body warm. His legs were cold but if he lay still the damp of the blanket mixed with a feverish sweat enclosed him in heat. Move, and a fit of shivering lasting minutes shook him to near exhaustion. Water patterned the floor and another patch had spread a dark map over the wall and the newly worked cement. It oozed through bricks, came up through stones by the door. The rain made such a noise.

Shadows around him changed shape, a gallery of familiar faces from the bar of The Bell closed over his head. Fires lit up the corner of the room. Flames danced on his bed and ate up the bedclothes. The faces smiled. One he could not recognise. If he concentrated he would remember. He was patient in the way he used to be. Pleased the stranger smiled at him. He took his hand. Taking his hand he saw it was light again, he was being dragged into the sun. It was someone he knew. He looked up and saw the crooked teeth of Melvyn.

The shepherd dragged him out to the wall where it was dry. He tried to stand, but rolled back wanting to sleep.

He was alone when next he woke. He had been moved by someone who had piled heather and dried fern around him. He remembered Mel Price he thought in a dream and wondered why it was dark so soon. Comfortable again he dreamed of heaven. He had been on a journey, gently supported, soothed by the voices softly calling that had led him to this familiar place. His mother spoke. He drank hot tea. He was lying in a soft bed. The policeman spoke to him. He felt pleased to see him.

'Clive,' he said remembering, 'we were at school.'

'You gave us all a headache when you disappeared.'

'I didn't disappear. Lynne will tell you.'

Lynne knew very little. Consumed with guilt she managed to keep her new boyfriend out of the way by saying she was ill and disappearing.

'I forbid you, absolutely forbid you – Edward support me – to go anywhere near that pub.' Sylvia Bailey took up a dominant position in front of a flower arrangement.

'Do you hear me?'

Elida pretended to sulk. In fact she was stimulated to the point of gaiety by the latest episode in a life she felt was partly hers. It made little change in her own joyless routine but her imagination took wing. She might never befriend this mysterious man but she dreamed of romantic scenes in which she might appear, intrigues in which she figured. She felt nothing for him but wished it were so.

'He's been sleeping rough. Did you know that?' her mother's voice broke through as she stood with him on a cliff at dawn.

'Oh dear!' Her father's reply was ambiguous. Elida escaped leaving husband and wife to come to another negative conclusion.

'Edward, dear.' He liked Ann Jerome's gravel tones in contrast to his wife's hard bite. Ann Jerome seemed to exhale a pot-pourri of fine dry scents that both soothed and sharpened like the sea. He could bathe in the flow, break and ebb of her mood. Ripples of her little laugh would stay with him after a good evening. Usually it involved the four of them. It was uncharacteristic of him to ruin his peace of mind and entertain Ann alone. Not that his wife's round of organised fun left notions of peace in its wake but it was a routine existence and suited him. It was at a routine dinner that chance made him look over the low range of flowers to the eyes of Ann that did not look away. Transfixed, a little thrill stayed his hand from the salt cellar where it wandered lost. He looked away and back. At the same time she lowered her eyes but the timing was slow and reassuring.

The Baileys were not an adventurous family. They would not roam. To go to a pub in another town was far enough and eating with Ann alone, he felt shipwrecked. It was not the conversation that disturbed him but the proximity of her dark eyes. And yet her composure and measured speech was matched by the control of the liquid eyes that stared at him sleeping and waking. He was trapped into lunch every Wednesday.

Suddenly fussy about his clothes his wife commented, 'Why do you want to change yourself? Are you having a crisis?'

Elida's friend cancelled, then re-invited herself, arrived, and from the first evening, took over. Such spirited plans, as going to pubs and smoking pot in the woods seemed shocking to Elida now. Little sensations of fear accompanied her thoughts and she worked hard to counter hints she had given over the telephone. Her friend, on the other hand, had already translated these ill-considered ideas into a way forward.

'Tomorrow at twelve, we'll have our first drink. What was the name of the pub?'

'Maddy,' even the name of her friend contained a threat, 'much better, lets drive to the coast!'

But Maddy was already ahead of her. 'Pub, Boys, Fun!' She posed by a mirror in anticipation. To Elida, the holiday was starting badly.

'How long is your friend staying?' Sylvia asked, sensing failure.

'I don't know.' Her daughter's tone like her father's could convey history. She sulked and read a book, hoping to quiet her wayward friend who mistook silence for success. The following day Maddy was 'damned' if she was 'wasting hours driving to the other side of Wales'. She had a brainwave which she explained bit by bit. The project was to track down the Maesford Man. Elida was bewildered by this. Distressed at the thought of causing more pain to someone she was secretly attracted to, she also experienced a fear that her mother had cultivated, of malign forces present on the hill. The more she thought her fear grew to the point of telling her mother. It had been years since she had talked to her mother as a friend. With her usual indecision she missed the moment and a row took place with Maddy. It started at dawn when her duvet was tweaked off and continued after breakfast.

'You go if you want to,' Elida exploded at last, 'I'm buggered if I am.' Her friend walked out of the house.

'It looks a bit rude.' Elida's mother observed niceties at all costs, but was glad to get rid of the girl. 'You really should have gone with her,' she sighed. Elida had a miserable day.

Maddy walked down to the town, excited by adventure. Elida was not 'cool'. Everybody knew, and she was better without her. But a free holiday was a plus, and for Maddy, fun was round every corner. The weather was unsettled. Rain came. She raced down the street, found the pub where they went the first day, bought sweet cider, crisps and chocolate and sat in a corner by the window away from the farmers. She was prepared to wait, but the waiting was torture. In one way she was relieved it was a girl and not Aledd behind the bar. She stood up. It would have been easier with a friend. Forcing a smile, she bought another cider, drank some of it. Too gassy, she put the glass down, pushed it away from her, made to leave and then a man came in. It was the one she expected. She was so pleased she felt grateful to him for being there. Her excitement returned and she made one of her prettier moves. He was waiting for his food; the girl at the bar had gone presumably to get it. When he turned, a glass in his hand, she was sitting at the first table.

'Can you tell me something?' She faked a blush as the shepherd stared. He was a man unused to conversation. Of Aledd's age, she supposed, but neglected oil on his overalls and cotton soldier's hat had made a young man old. Yuck, she thought, his teeth missing. He looked away with the shy move of a loner, then back, quite sweet, she thought. His eyes were dark. He put the glass down while he considered her face and hair – contrived to look matted. All the while she was speaking hesitantly with smiles and laughs. Eventually he sat down when his food arrived. As she talked, her voice light as a whisper, he did not take his eyes from her face.

'You must eat,' she said, 'it'll be cold.'

'Don't go there alone,' he said.

'No,' she laughed, 'I'll come with you.' She laughed again. 'Just as far as the ridge. I know it quite well. I often stay here with my friend.'

The shepherd put down his knife and fork again, his eyes on her hair.

'You want to come on my buggy?'

'Five minutes,' she said.

They did not speak again.

'You'll be all right?' He had dropped her as promised. She did not persuade him further, escaping with many thanks.

'What a tale,' she said in her head as she imagined herself back tucked up in bed at the Baileys.

As the sound of the engine softened in the distance she was bolder now, alone in the temperate afternoon, hills gently spreading. She would go on – the shepherd perhaps still within call – and, finding the stone pile that the Maesford Man was known to have claimed, peep in. But the shepherd was gone. All at once she saw or thought she saw a hole in the distance set in the hill's cleft or something unnameable. She had to know, drew closer. It was the place, a hovel, silent and empty. Through cracks shone a pale sun. She looked and shrank away. It had got darker. Scared, she half ran, uncertain of the way back. It seemed lighter again. She got a lift and, with the town in sight, didn't care, safe or unsafe. She said little that night, hiding her considerable tiredness under a languid manner.

'Seems to have slowed her down,' mother whispered to daughter.

'Well?' Elida asked later. And much later in the night she listened, admiration hidden by the dark. In her friend's description she pictured a scene richer than anything she had imagined and was given the knowledge she wanted without an effort on her part. In the blackness she questioned where was the window, where was the door.

Silent except for the cropping and clattering of sheep, the

building sweated and soaked up rain. In places the mortar held, in others it powdered to a pink dust. Moisture mottled the rag bed. Metal containers gave way to rust. The plastic roof sheets slit by the buffeting wind, rustled from time to time, jagged edges like dead leaves moved by a lift in the heavy air. Three walls remained, the fourth was a bank of stones.

Windows had once overlooked the lower plain and mountains, left and right, and a gully, hedged and ditched, ran down hill dividing the terrain. In the main wall of the hovel, a door made for some larger frame, rough cut to size, swung inwards on a broken hinge letting in triangles of light with shafts of rain onto wet rubble. Opposite was a chimney and below the makings of a fire. To anyone looking in, it bore the mark of someone living there. Whatever her friend had seen or made up, Elida imagined it in detail as she lay in her warm painted bed.

Next day she waved to her departing friend and relaxed for the first time that summer.

His mother knew the silent stare would soon turn to tears of boredom, but the hour's drive to Maddy's home had passed agreeably with maternal comments from Sylvia bringing polite responses from the girls, who ate cream teas and thanked her for her trouble in quite a surprising way. The drive back to Hill House was interminable but unstrained, celebrated by a meal cooked by Edward who looked flushed. It was a short evening, unbroken sleep. The Baileys felt at peace again. They were not an adventurous family.

The doctor had something to say about young people who thought they could live like 'hippies', a description that had stayed with him since strange persons dressed in yellow had come to the village some years ago. Primitive cottages and dangerous mountain pools also appeared on the agenda for public discussion. In the weeks that followed Aledd's bout of fever, he recalled the driving out of demons quoted in the vicar's text that week, and demons it would appear had driven Aledd to frenzy. 'Relax, boy,' he said, 'your mother can do the driving and make you stop. I see you're back at the farm again. Good.'

Aledd had had a strange experience. 'Unlike me!' He laughed

as he threw logs on the family fire, kept burning even in summer.

'You were bad,' his mother said, and said no more on the subject. 'Help your father.'

Together they cut and stacked wood while his father swore at his arthritis, ate tea, silently planned the next day, secure in the knowledge that the future was fixed. Maesford, the old Maesford, was unlike the Maesford of the Town. Wealth had built a termite's nest, and as easily destroyed, some would say. The old world was still with them although the village community had gone. Aledd felt it in the land he worked. His ideas he had inherited, unconcerned that others had turned to the shining world he saw each time he looked up to the lights on the hill. He seemed to forget he was once drawn there, and the excitement. Today he was content to hear the fire snap as he threw on a log, and watch the dog as it slept, and his father, old thoughts darkening his face, and his mother, still stacking plates in the kitchen, wiping the plastic cloth with a rhythmic movement that calmed him. He felt for a moment he was back, a child again, listening to the familiar sounds of a childhood haven.

The next day he walked up to the town, past the shops he would never go into, gift shops, clothes shops for the swinging young or country clothes for matrons. Back from the road, a new Roman Catholic church, its architecture angled in all directions, opened its doors to a departing pink-faced priest who gave Aledd a 'Good morning, my son' with such a grin and nod he wondered if he dared look inside. It was cool and wet and he wished himself in the mountains. He looked down at the old shop just visible at the foot of the hill, scene of his contrary fortunes. It had been for sale for more than a year and never sold. 'Asking too much,' they said and he was sure it was true.

'People like that'll start another business, you'll see.'

This sort of remark made him sad in a way he could not explain and he would turn away. A firm drizzle was forming a mist in the valley and low cloud would soon cut off the mountain peaks. On an impulse he set off away from the town, the damp like a bandage round his head, down and then towards the far hills across the marsh. There was a river where the water seemed to pipe a tune as it funnelled through a hollow and spread over stones. It sang to him and the big water birds, grey as rocks. He had come home, it told him. Not to the farm and family, not to love but to that other place. He was strong again and scrambled up the steep slopes.

The place was staring at him. He was sorry he had neglected it for so long. He started to clear the floor again, patiently this time, no more driven by anxiety than a desire to create something and prove himself. The shepherd was loitering on his buggy. Lighter than a tractor it rolled weightlessly over the ground. Today it appeared like a big beast. He waved and Aledd acknowledged.

'Hey.' Aledd had not had a conversation with him for years. They exchanged a salute sometimes over a meal at The Bell or down at The Black Ox.

'Mel,' he continued. The man seemed startled that Aledd knew his name.

'I'm better.' Aledd spoke in answer to something unsaid.

'Back?' The shepherd indicated the old shack.

'Private. Just for me.'

It was raining hard by the time he got home. He thought his mother would ask questions but she said nothing. He settled with the dog by the fire again. A fire was the one comfort in the hill farms and more entertaining, Aledd maintained, even when struggling with extra firings at work. The flames were dying down to a bed of red ash. It looked like a sunset.

'Get more wood.' His father's voice reminded him he was in his father's chair. He started guiltily, and found wood and spent a long time sawing in the shed.

Edward feared Wednesday would give him another ulcer. He tried to dress 'down' in case Sylvia noticed. He made his exit in a spray of dust from the drive. His wife looked up, went to the door and made an irritated clicking sound at the tyre marks. She felt disturbed by unusual marks and sounds.

'Elida?' The voice seemed unnaturally loud.

'Yes, what is it?' said her daughter, cross.

'Nothing. I just wondered what everyone was doing, that's all.' She sighed, but with a sense of relief went back to her telephoning.

Twenty miles in another county, Ann was seated in her usual place. Her presence both calmed and at the same time tensed Edward. 'The news?' The Jeromes were not much interested in local affairs, continually leaving for another address before they had time to focus.

'There is a public meeting,' her purring voice went on. 'We can't go, but you must. And tell us all about it. As you know, John refused from the day we arrived to have anything to do with local politics. He's spent a lifetime being treasurer on boards, church of course, and now he wants to rest and I don't blame him.'

'No.' Edward like her was in confidential mood which never exceeded the bounds of their personal world. 'No,' he whispered again. He hoped sympathy went without saying.

'It seems there are things in the town that need clearing up. Not just the town, but happenings around us that are beginning to affect our lives.'

Edward curled his foot round his crossed leg in anticipation. 'Yes,' he said.

'Two things concerning the council are to be raised by us – private citizens – you do agree, don't you?'

'Yes,' he said.

'Derelict houses, dangerous pools or lakes. I suppose it doesn't really matter to us. I don't even know where these places are. But there are people.' Her eyes are pools or lakes, he thought. 'You know who I mean, don't you?'

He tried to return to her present preoccupation. 'Yes.'

'People are involved who work for us or have contact with us, in hotels and shops. And you have a young daughter. The proposal is... pull down the buildings, barns... fill in the pools. Perhaps the health authority...'

It was up to Edward to offer another view before agreeing with her. Farmers, animals and preservation of rural life were touched on so lightly that by the time the countryside came up, her mind was in Norfolk.

'Of course, the countryside – we shall be heading for Burnham Thorpe.' They were nearly through their sandwiches and into the dregs of a wine bottle.

'Edward, you are naughty. That wine looks expensive.'

He beamed as she took him down the motorway to another land. 'Coffee?' She declined and was off, waving from the car. She never looked where she was going. He supposed she felt fate protected her because of her special insurances. He drove idly home to find Ann's car in his drive.

'I was telling Sylvia,' she said, 'you must go to this meeting.'

She was amazing, he thought as her voice rolled out the words he had heard less than an hour before. His eyes fixed on hers in surprise. She knew no guilt. She could probably lie and confirmed what he knew the first time she had looked at him that night across the dinner table. He and she had a relationship. The thought of love made him tremble.

'That man's back in town,' Sylvia said from the kitchen.

Aledd had another job. The owners of The Black Ox, once an old farm at the bottom of the town on the edge of the original village enclosure, decided to give the business one more chance. With the lease running out it could easily be sold as a private dwelling. Constructed around a property razed by fire a century ago there remained a large baking oven, the only clue to its former life. It was a feature. Every year they ensured a large log the size of a bench was placed in the hearth. Sat upon in summer, from October to March it burned, stoked by smaller wood, a mound of ash glowing below. A round table with four chairs took up a central position for four ancients. Although little more than middle aged they were deemed the four wise men and formed a virtual blockade to visitors who were forced to drink in bar number two. The threat of losing their fire had made them querulous. The air had become tense. On entering a stranger faced waves of hostility. In defence he would return to the street and in future pass by on the other side of the road.

To save the day Aledd was employed with his smile and fresh-air face and took up his position each morning behind the bar.

'The Vaughan boy,' they murmured, their ritual preserved. And he became an actor again, flicked a duster, coughed as he chased away insects, watched with pleasure as his stage filled.

'I know the people here, Owen, Glen, John...' He raked the fire and smoke filled the air in a way nobody minded. The first day six people came in. He seemed to forget the experiences of the summer. In this new world of dark interiors it became his mission to let in some light. He leaned out of the window in the bar number two and looked up and down the street. It was quiet except for a few cars. He took to doing this whenever the place was empty. It gave him position. It was not an attractive area. It was not where people would expect to find him, which made it amusing. He was given paint and set about decorating. Brown walls became white and flowers in a vase at the window changed most days thanks to the throw outs from a market garden. He sat beside them, curled like a cat. There was little else to do but wait for someone to walk down the street. He waited for two or three days but she never came. At first he didn't want her to appear. It was so nice anticipating. He had waited a fourth and fifth day when he got a letter.

'Dear Aledd,' it stated formally. 'It's terrible. They are going to pull down the cottage.' He thought of the shepherd's hut at first, then his hideaway, but no one knew of it.

'I feel desperate. We must do something. Please meet me there the next fine evening. I hope you don't hate me after all that's happened. We were happy. I still love you.' The name 'Lynne' was given a halo of kisses and a line underneath. He finished work and mad with joy, went home only to tell his mother he was gardening and he was off in the van, used sparingly now.

He drove fast but the engine noise slowed him. Rattling along heads turned.

'He gets around,' one said.

'He don't stay down for long.'

Skidding in the dust and small puddles that were always present, his hopes were up. He considered parking a distance from the cottage but as he climbed higher to the first line of hills it didn't seem to matter. Why, he asked himself, should anything matter now? Life had turned around and he was back in the world, himself again. Who would not be pleased for him – for them both – Mel the shepherd, Clive the policeman. Even the doctor had once carried a message from his beloved, albeit only to turn him down. It was odd, he thought, he was happier free of her. Oh, well, that was then. Things had changed. He should reach the cottage first. As he approached, anxiety took away his breath. But at the gate, with no unwelcome signs, he jumped from the van. Before he pushed through the half open ruin of a door, he peered through a window, his hands around his face. The door handle turned and gave at a touch; he looked back at the town he had just left. That too was beautiful, he thought, and went in.

He kicked dirty blankets aside. It was horrible and at the same time good. He stopped clearing up as memory overwhelmed him. He pictured good and beautiful days. Now he saw himself as she would see him, in dirt stained clothes. Nothing must spoil this day. He went outside and scanned the lane and hill tracks. There was no sign of her. Like his window watching at the pub, it was both a pleasure and a pain. Today it was more than pleasure, it was intoxicating knowing she would come. He was content for time to go by. An hour passed. He would wait no longer. He had waited and the idea that she might not come choked him. The dull beat of his heart forced him to accept his fate. Alone he considered all the valid reasons that had kept her from him. His spirits that all day had sent him spinning to reach this point – the valley seemed to darken now even as he looked at it – had gone with his spent breath. It had gone, wherever it was. He had been right before. He should never have had any more to do with her. She had punished him once and would do again. His throat ached. Angrily he crashed through the door.

She was level with the van. Watching her out of breath, he felt tears in his eyes. He picked her up and carried her in and placed her gently on the rag bed, turned over, wept. Now he was laughing, sat up. She stared at him.

'You're crazy,' she said. 'I thought we'd split up.'

'No,' he said.

'I'm not going to start again. It made me ill. Don't spoil it.'

'I won't spoil it. We'll do anything you like.'

'I don't want to do anything. Can't we just sit here?'

'Yes. I said, anything you like.' After a while he said, 'Are you happy?'

'No,' she said, 'I'm miserable.'

'I'm so happy.' He sat up and looked at her. 'It's you.' He

kissed her quietly until she seemed to like it.

'Don't make me do it,' she said as he kissed her more. 'Don't make me do it,' she said from time to time in the darkness as he slowly took off her clothes, familiar curves and buttons and broken zip. 'No,' the voice was so quiet, he could hardly hear her. Whatever she said, he knew it would never stop this wonderful moment of his. He said the words as she lay pretending to sleep.

'Can't you be happy?' he asked later. 'It was wrong of me.' But she was not speaking. He collected her up like a child and put her in the van.

'You're getting me mixed up,' he said as they drove in silence. 'I was so happy and you were so sad. What have I done?' He said in despair. 'Tell me what I have done.'

'Nothing. It's me,' was all she said.

'Did you walk?' She nodded.

'The cottage was still here for us. You wanted that?'

He dropped her near her home. As she turned in the van headlamps, there were bruises on her face he hadn't noticed before. He stayed awake that night and at dawn waited outside her house. He was afraid of her father, but more afraid she would go from him again and this time for ever. She ran past the car. He pulled away from the kerb, parked again and following on foot continued behind her slowly, drawing level as her pace relaxed.

'I won't do this again. I'll go but tell me.'

'I'm so mixed up.'

'Why are you so unhappy?'

'I can't tell you.' Holding her, he felt her hand unclasp.

He did the thing he least expected of himself and set her free. It seemed he had said 'goodbye'. There was no one to hear them. No words said. No sound but her feet light on the road in parting. He called her name but she didn't turn. He called to her defiant back, 'If we were friends, you'd tell me.' He watched her up the hill approaching the shops, blocks of buildings of different size hiding her and then she would appear again climbing steps to a door.

Where she was going he had no right to know. He was nothing to her. Late for work. He might get the sack. Time had moved on while he stood still. He was in another world. People were waiting. They shuffled uncertainly up to the bar. With an effort he managed to speak. What he said would have no meaning.

'I am buying you all a drink,' and, with forced enthusiasm, 'it's a special day.'

He spent the time lighting the fire that stubbornly smouldered. Soon the four from the farm settled down.

'Going to the meeting, then?'

Aledd presumed the words were addressed to him. 'I hadn't heard about one.'

'I'd 'a thought you'd 'a known.'

The voice sounded casual. In his new role he found the strength to soak up trouble. He needed information and boldly continued.

'Why me?'

'You and that cottage up there.'

'Oh that! It's not mine any more.'

They paused to smoke, bending under the match flame to murmur a name.

'Lent to me once.' Aledd covered any reaction by swabbing the chalked menu board. Water trickled in grey lines.

'Messy business,' he heard from the fire.

Daring all, his reputation at stake he said, 'It was my girlfriend, you see. She didn't like it.' The same voice growled an answer he took to be sympathetic.

Every day he waited for her to come but she never appeared. It was not the sort of place for a girl. He changed things round again, irritating the men, sat in the window ignoring remarks. He liked to see people. The Bailey girl went by and stared at him. He waved and he thought she smiled.

It was possible to be the object of gossip and be convinced people were talking of somebody else. It needed a detail to be wrong to give peace of mind and anonymity. He was amused to hear his old haunts referred to as 'Black' and 'Magic'. People from abroad came there, they said, with bad city ways. Combined with a newcomer's suspicion that country folk drew forces from the earth, and fed violence into the mountains, there was a will to find evidence of something dark and supernatural. Someone had seen animal bones and fur and bloodstains on the heather, flattened areas, a stone like an altar and a cross of charred wood. Remembering his attempts at bean rows, Aledd laughed. Until he grimly thought of strangers trampling his garden. This was more worrying as he had another secret. For a week he woke in the night, agitated until he realised his other shack, the one that concealed his treasure, was far enough out in the wilderness. Soon, he devised a plan either to destroy or bury the evidence.

In search of decoration for the bar he had been given books by neighbours to be placed along the shelves between the horse brasses. Poetry books with tooled covers appealed to him most and one day he read one. It was part of the charm of the job to look or read and have hours to please himself. He settled to read narrative poems. He liked the repeated chorus. One in particular fascinated him and he returned to it again and again. 'Oh my sweet Basil,' the lady cried, mourning her lover whose skull would one day emerge through the herbs. He could grow basil, once he knew what it was, and his secret would be buried safe. His pots soon became a feature, one in the pub and one at the farm. He switched them around to encourage growth.

'Photosynthesis,' he explained. 'On the farm, one learns things.'

The meeting chaired by Gerald Weatherstone, MP was not well attended. Faced with empty seats, some men would sense failure, but Gerald was going in to battle. He moved his army forward and, shoulder-to-shoulder, each face became an acquaintance that formerly had no name.

'We few,' he said, with more reference to war, and outlined his plan.

The Baileys were there and a doctor partially retired who now had time for people. The Jeromes sent their house sitters. Sylvia didn't know them and worried about the correct manner of approach. In front was a woman who might buy her shop. A landowner sent a bailiff. He arrived with wife, sister and brother-in-law. The policeman stayed ten minutes. A few others were of no significance to Sylvia. The vicar was late, his wife later.

'I thought we were to discuss the subject of Satanism,' a female voice rose from the hall.

'Nonsense,' and 'what did she say?' came back in answer down the rows. It was not quite the subject on the agenda but Gerald Weatherstone, with a politician's sense of theatre, took over just as the Rev. Ben Tooley was coming through the door.

'What do you say, Vicar?'

As he was out of breath he said nothing, sat heavily on a chair, gasped, forced himself to stand again, moved forward a few paces, turned, moved backwards some more before addressing the congregation finally.

'I believe,' he said, 'in the power of good over evil. We are all tools.'

'Especially Mrs Tooley,' called a wag from the crowd.

'Oh, do be quiet,' said Sylvia after a rumble of laughter.

The vicar started an apology. 'I'm sorry. I'm the last to arrive.' He wasn't. His wife at this point slid into an isolated chair left by the doorman who had gone for a smoke.

'Nearly the last.' He was determinedly light-hearted and laughed. The crowd laughed too and settled down for an entertainment. 'We need your views, but first the facts.'

'Now then.' Gerald took control. 'Let us consider the evidence. I have here a list of complaints. As I read them raise a hand if anyone has first-hand knowledge.' Someone giggled. He had not intended a joke. 'The list before me is rather colourful. I am aware that people's imaginations can run riot. Yes!' An unknown citizen was standing.

'Rivers of blood,' Sylvia whispered to her husband.

'Flashing lights. You can see them from here. Lights on the mountains. There are people there. There's no road but there are people. If you look now.' The voice became a whisper in conversation with someone behind.

'Squatters,' called the postman's wife. No longer a neighbour of the noisy Marchells she was happy to silence their pert girl Lynne.

'New age travellers will be coming.' This was news to them all.

'New age travellers have not been seen in this area,' Gerald went on. 'I have noticed perhaps two horse-drawn caravans. I believe they are holiday hires. They all look far too clean.'

'Not the children,' from the back.

'They move on. We have all seen them by the roadside. One night and they are off.'

'Not the children,' the voice went on, 'they increase overnight.'

'Representing Green Peace, we support...'

'Vicar!'

'Here you may like to reflect,' the vicar drank from a glass of water, 'on peace.' The Rev. Ben Tooley was on firm ground. 'We thrive. I need you, sir! Yes, the gentleman who has just spoken!' and who at this point had reached the exit no doubt to fly a green flag over the Border. 'It is wonderful. We are Green to a man.'

'Generally,' murmured Gerald.

'Little green men,' came back the needling voice.

'Let me stop you,' interrupted Gerald firmly for the first time. Good at crowd control, he had no fears from twenty people but UFO's were stretching it.

There were two people who liked a stage, Gerald and the vicar. Seeing him as an ally and conscious of the weight of the church, having newly arrived from town to country, Gerald urged the Rev. Ben Tooley onto the platform amid clapping. They stood together like schoolmasters on a rugby line and went to work.

'A good beginning.'

'A new society.'

Cries of 'Name, name...' from the floor. After suggestions, 'Watch-works' was popular while 'Virtual Watch' was ruled out because, as someone said, 'You don't really have to do it.'

Talk was becoming foolish. Gerald closed the meeting with his 'Good Start' speech and handed the night to the vicar. 'Off you go,' he concluded heartily, 'and, as they say in Bridge, or rather I don't say, my wife plays, I don't, as you know, yes, off you go and...' he got to the point at last, '...length is not strength! That's it.' People were standing, someone had opened the door and dust was blowing in. 'Thank you and see you in church,' Gerald concluded.

'When will it end?' Edward Bailey mused. His wife had taken root. 'What's she planning now?' He feared her thoughts.

'I hope you'll all come back to the vicarage for coffee,' the vicar's wife sighed.

Sylvia Bailey determined to go to church more regularly.

They left like a rustle of leaves.

'A week today – in your diaries,' called Sylvia from a lectern. She moved sideways, grabbing Gerald's arm. 'You can come to us, of course.'

Edward, reckless on the brink of romance, put it to him, 'Drinks with us or coffee with the vicar.'

'Shut up, Edward.' Sylvia edged to the door. People were following the vicar. 'Gerald, I may call you Gerald, mayn't I? Can you come for a drink?'

'I really think I am the vicar's man for the moment.'

'Yes, of course. Oh vicar.' Sylvia never missed a chance. 'Can't you come to us... no? Of course you can't, another time then.'

Jemima Weatherstone liked to paint. With this in mind, Gerald with more than his usual confidence had his plan laid. His stance spoke authority.

'Here,' he said, one foot on the log box. 'Pack up! We're on Safari!'

'Oh no!'

'Oh, yes, we're off to the hills. Painting your favourite place,' he added, using an American rising inflection. After a year in the States he had the notion that America meant business and anything transatlantic could move mountains, in this case his wife.

'The children,' she countered in case he had forgotten them.

'Out,' he said. 'We'll take the Range Rover. I'm thinking of beer and cheese and you can paint when you are tired of walking.'

Jemima had spent miserable hours in her husband's hill climbing days being more at home on studio couches.

'I haven't tuned in,' she said.

'Now's your chance.'

With the Art Society's choice of the year, not hers, hung on the walls of their rented house, she was sulky. Her husband's voice trailed on.

'I'm going to take a look to establish once and for all any sense or nonsense in these rumours. And I need you with me for your opinion.'

'You never want my opinion.'

'I do now. Come on, be mystic. Experience forces, if there are any. I mean it.'

She was laughing at him. 'I don't believe you,' she shrieked, mocking.

'You should hear them in the town. Evil, they will tell you!'

Seeing a flicker of interest, he knew he had won. The only bad aspect he could see was the inaccessibility of the place. The tracks plunged into mud-soaked beds, sometimes drying out in an altitude of fierce winds to form hard ridges two-feet deep. Keeping the car tyres above the hollows with a firm grip on the wheel, it was possible to make progress but this became increasingly difficult as the heather gave way to fern and grass and the vehicle angled acutely. He had slowed enough for Jemima to act. He knew what she was up to. She had shifted her position across through the opening door.

'Don't! I need your weight.' He had spoken too late. The car rocked. She was on the ground. 'This is supposed to balance even at sharp angles,' he complained uselessly.

'I think you've passed that point,' she said, reaching for the paint box she had brought with her.

He moved forward a few feet and pulled up. She slid down a bank, considered for a moment, sat and started to paint. Her actions were inexplicable.

'Unbelievable,' he said aloud, getting out of the car himself. 'I'm walking.'

'Don't be long, it's bloody winter,' she called after him. The heat had gone out of the sun and a cloud the size of a carpet came and went.

He was walking in the direction, he hoped, of the infamous 'Mawn Pool' when he heard thunder. He stopped. It was coming from two directions. He looked to the hill above. Advancing like a wave came a number of sheep, behind them came more, running, and beyond them more, possibly hundreds, heading down the track. He climbed back onto the heather. There was no dog, no man, just sheep in a surge like a river.

He had escaped just in time. He saw in the weight of numbers he could have been knocked down. He was about to face the hill again when a slick of water no more than a cupful spilt by an unseen hand, appeared before him in the path. It was a mystery. Like the hill it seemed to grow in front of him. Then he saw it was seeping through the heather. Thunder, more thunder rolled around him and then the rain. A runnel of water, coming from the path above and high up in the mountains hidden by cloud, had become a rolling stream. Falling in straight lines, the rain was deafening. He had heard rain on pavements but this was a roar. Water beat in his ears and face, rain wrapped around his legs. He felt helpless. There was one thought in his mind as he fought against this overwhelming beast – get back to the car. When he reached it, it was on its side in a trench where water had caused deep erosions in the earth. Jemima had gone. In the mud were some paints.

He was more concerned about the car. Stuck here no one would steal it, a farmer might tow it away, they must come around regularly. He had seen vehicles crawling across precipitous slopes. Would they perhaps dump it down the bank? He walked angrily towards a group of corrugated iron constructions in a valley. A man, more amused than surprised came with his son and righted the precious machine now with mud on the windows, and he was able to drive off. He made a note to thank the farmer in a more tangible way. He had been unexpectedly kind. 'Not the first,' the man had said and wagged his head knowingly.

Gerald Weatherstone thought of his wife as he drove on firmer ground and could resume a political style. Home by now, he imagined and relieved to be out of this godforsaken place. He looked back to see the menacing country as soft and ordered as a quilt spread in careful design for sheep and the great birds that circled overhead. Not a place to live in he thought as he put as many miles as he could in the time it took him to feel civilised again.

'Where the hell is Jemima?' He was anxious again as neat trees mocked his plight down a well planted road. More worried about his son left with a neighbour, he headed for home. His wife always survived. Sometimes it was better without her. In his head, he prepared a speech for the evening. He was late all round. He'd take the other car, boring but clean. He hated being late. Once his anger subsided, he realised he was tired.

He took the meeting without his usual enthusiasm. When asked for ideas on subjects last described as urgent, he was restrained, even reticent. When pressed, he was content to mediate.

'A level-headed view,' he said, 'could serve the community better than any extreme action by Church.' Here he was to mention Bell, Book & Candle and razing buildings to the ground, but that might displease. 'Demolition of property in a land with a housing shortage is not an option.'

'The cottage beyond the plains is condemned,' announced the farm bailiff, to a chorus of surprise.

'Dear Ben,' he wrote – the vicar was not able to be there – 'I think we may congratulate ourselves on the meeting in Maesford Town Hall on 20 September. As before, a small group showed a genuine and positive attitude, so necessary in this new venture. Important to take the steps we proposed to take.'

A sound distracted him, a cow in some vile predicament, what else! Stopping, he found his mind had wandered. His wife had not returned. He was worried about the bloody woman. What decisions were they taking? He could hardly remember summing up. The place was affecting his mind.

'I have taken it upon myself to visit the areas of concern and now have a better idea of the situation. With advice to visitors on precautions...' He got up and phoned Sylvia Bailey. The answerphone spoke to him at some length. Fascinated he forgot to replace his receiver and next found he was recording a message.

'Phone tonight if you can.'

He hung up as a car drew up, not Jemima but his two wet children with a patient neighbour.

'Wet,' she said unnecessarily.

He sent them upstairs with two ice creams to change or something. He heard them moving about, but the house was peculiarly quiet without his wife. He was used to her absences, but this time she had not so much left as seemingly been spirited away.

He continued writing, 'Leaving dangerous buildings in the hands of local officials who after all have had long associations with the countryside will be a more practical solution. The same goes for waterlogged ground.' He had not got anywhere near the sinister 'Mawn Pool', neither did he intend to. He remembered Sylvia's offer of whisky again and poured himself a drink. Switching on the television, he had forgotten much of his troubled day until the picture began its dance. The reception was weak in the town, some channels unattainable, others would snow or die. He tried Sylvia's number again, regretted it and replaced the receiver before she or the answerphone cut in. He was not going to the police about Jemima, he was quite determined.

'What a cow,' he said aloud again. It was becoming a habit with him. Combined with an indecision that never troubled him before, he blamed the borderlands – neither one thing nor the other. His restlessness got him from his chair to pour a second whisky.

After an unsatisfactory phone call to her friend, Elida Bailey wrote a letter which was to precipitate her into a world more uncertain than anything she had imagined from the seclusion of the house. Discussing delicate matters from her changing points of view, a split had developed in a school friendship and she would need to mend it.

Hill House
Maesford

Dear Maddy,

After you have read this burn it. I know you think I am making it up but what I said about the other thing was a fact. I am not kidding. I know where it is and I can prove it. I panicked the other day but tomorrow I am meeting someone who will take me to the place I told you about. I'll get the stuff, trust me.

Love,

Elida

Once this was sent she knew what she must do. Written it must be posted. Once posted she must enter the town. Each step of the process frightened her, knowing it was out of character. Her character shamed her and she would change it. If she could change once, she could be a different person. Repetition would perfect it like learning a part.

'Are you ill?' asked her mother. 'You look green. There's someone at the door. I must go.'

Elida escaped.

'Gerald, how nice.'

'I'm taking you up on your invitation, a day late, I'm afraid. But the vicar is so keen I felt I must go back with him and establish…'

'Yes, come on in.' Sylvia showed him into the drawing room with a fire, and shut the door.

Elida found a stamp in the study and, guilty as a thief, slipped out of the house. Running shook body and mind. She felt better reaching the post. Running home she felt worse. The task she had set herself was too difficult to contemplate. She would wait a day and, when her will was strong, she would pretend she was that other person. As she returned, the visitor was leaving. She must have been out for an hour. She shivered.

'Stay longer next time,' her mother was saying. Sylvia was stimulated enough to take her daughter into her confidence.

'We're all going on a tour of inspection. Here's the map.' Someone had made a photocopy of several miles of hillside, enlarged and pencilled with points of interest.

'You can come. You'd like that. After we've worked out a route.'

Elida felt the world changing. 'Yes,' she agreed.

Into the town and down the hill in a new top she had changed twice, Elida started a new life. As she approached The Ox, she lost heart. He was cleaning the window and waved. She had to go in.

'Can I have coffee?' The board on the pavement advertising tea had been her inspiration.

'Yes,' Aledd smiled. She found him magnetic as his colour rose. She sat awkwardly on the bar stool. There was no one else around and she knew she looked tense.

'Like it in the other side? Nicer there.' Aledd had saved her. She was so relieved after the darkness of the bar, she gave a giggle of gratitude. The room, pretty as a teashop, was bathed by a pale sun in lemon light. Relaxed she touched a bright ceramic vase and smiled, pleased with her adventure.

He brought in coffee and a cake and, remembering her mission, she was tense again. Her hand shook as she held the cup. She hoped he hadn't noticed. He was too busy, she supposed, arranging things in the room, opening and closing a cupboard door that seemed to be stuffed with papers. There was silence again except for a rumble of sounds from the bar, clicks and words and footsteps tapping. She had the notion she was alone and free for the first time, nobody knew or cared who she was. Liberated she became brave and crossed the room, scrutinising old photos – local people perhaps, and views. Boldly she opened the cupboard. Papers spilled out. Replacing them, she found more pictures, flyblown and caked with tobacco-smoke but a treasure trove someone had discarded. Appalled by her curiosity, her mother would have fits, she stuffed things back, bent at the corners. At the window table she waited again, but had lost her appetite. She wondered what to do next. If she stood in the doorway he would remember she was there, but any attention from the farmers would scare her. She went to the cupboard again. When discovered she would apologise and, using her mother's party manner, enthuse over the pictures.

'I'm sorry,' she said when he eventually returned. 'It's rude of me to look. I couldn't resist it.'

'You haven't had a cake.' He was over at the table.

'No, I was more interested in the room.'

'It may have got dry.' He was more concerned with catering. 'I keep them in a tin to stop them going hard... or soft, but this one must have escaped.' He made her smile again.

'It's all right. I love old photos, though.'

'Oh, those old things,' he said without interest as he wrote out a bill on the smallest of writing pads. '90p,' he continued, handing it to her.

She skipped out into the street. She had done it. She had achieved something all her own and entered the world.

The next week she came most days to sit in the window seat with her coffee. It was pleasant and she felt grown-up.

'Can I ask you something?' she said one morning.

He had started sitting at her table and smoking a cigarette, which he kept hidden in odd places, in between books and magazines.

'Do you know where...?' It was hard to keep going. She started again.

'Someone said they used to grow cannabis in the mountains.' He didn't answer. She blushed and looked at her hands. In the silence when she dared look up again he was smiling easily, relaxed in the cigarette smoke.

'There is so much gossip.' He blew out a warm cloud.

'Well...' She listened only to his voice, grateful for a mood unchanged despite her interruption. He must be a kind man, she thought.

'People will tell you,' he was saying, 'there are miles of hillside where nothing grows. Even the sheep graze past it some of the year. Just bracken, it's just bracken.'

'But I thought you knew about it. Everybody knows.'

'Everybody doesn't know. If anybody did they wouldn't tell you. That's what I mean.'

'They say you know. You grow it.'

He did not react.

'It's so silly to criticise. Some people drink, some people smoke. It's silly to criticise.'

'Not silly.' He had changed his position very slightly in shadow.

'I'm sorry,' she said.

'Why sorry?' His stillness frightened her. They seemed cast in stone. Time must have passed. He was standing a few steps away occupied with the furniture. 'Promise me something.' His voice was cool. Elida did not move.

'I'm not saying these things don't exist.' He paused. 'You're young; you don't know where these things can lead. Your mother and I have had our differences but I don't want her to think – or anyone for that matter – that I encouraged you to do anything illegal. It is illegal, you know.' She was ready to cry.

51

'It's funny!' He could laugh in different ways, now it was teasing. 'You refused the cake because you were leaving and here you are still, me talking. If you don't want it now, take it home. My mother made it.' He wrapped it in several paper napkins. 'Free,' he said and thrust it in her hand. She left as quickly as she could.

The old shop, the background of his youth it seemed to Aledd, had released onto the market certain collectable objects that Farnaby's, a respected antique shop, would normally despise. In the name of change they had introduced certain items into the window area in what was considered a light-hearted way. It was not a shop that Aledd would have frequented. He found the pale face of the owner forbidding and the objects expensive but encouraged by the new display he went inside. In hallowed darkness where corners concealed mysteries, there might just be a container for his garden. He always knew what he wanted. He spotted an iron cauldron and asked the price. Ignoring the answer he wondered aloud where he could find another one.

'We can always get another.' The man was bored. He did not see this rustic as a customer.

'It's for a private house.'

Sensing a deal, life returned to the shopkeeper. 'It might not be an exact match but it would correspond, as it were, for flowers. A charming change from the usual tubs.'

'I'll call back. I'm always passing.' Aledd had no idea how he would pay for it but he would save his wages. His confidence soared. What a present for his mother, for Lynne. What prestige. If it was too much. He could always say no, but for the first time Mr Farnaby had spoken to him. He was established in his own eyes as a citizen, a competitor. Within weeks he would have bought himself position. He drove slowly in the van, leaning back with his arms stretched out holding the top of the wheel. He glanced in the mirror to see if he had changed.

One day he was to clatter with his pots full of earth to his bedroom.

'What are you about?' His mother had watched him digging in different parts of the garden to find soil.

'Dirt all upstairs.'

'It's a surprise, Mam!'

'Not a surprise I like.' His mother was more talkative that evening.

'You're late. Food'll be cold. Dad's legs are bad. Food'll settle them.'

She placed a foot heavily on the stair. Soot slid from the paper he was holding. He must have left a trail from the barn where an old chimney concealed his secrets. He pushed the soot under the bed with the pots. There was still soot and some earth on the floor.

They were all in good spirits once food had got to his father's legs. Luck was with him for a while. That night he dragged out the pots again and in one, rearranged the earth over a large tobacco tin.

'What's this here?' His mother had found more evidence. He huddled very still with his knees up on the bed like a child fearing discovery.

He took the pots to the pub.

'Nothing grows this time of year.'

'Yes they will, they're herbs.'

'Herbs, where'd you get herbs?'

'Ahh!' he replied.

The pots gave him confidence. He went to see the farmer who had once lent him the cottage. He strolled with his casual actor's air to the market garden where he found him on a tractor.

'Sorry, boy, but I was under pressure,' he said at last, referring to the cottage.

'I know,' said Aledd. 'It didn't matter.'

'Well, I felt a bit bad.'

'What plants'll do this time of year?'

'Nothing'll do this time of year.'

'Not indoors?'

'I dunno, try ivy.'

Sylvia Bailey's new idea would bear the name 'Party Planner'. A bright sign lay on the kitchen table. The letters in alternate colours gave it a flash look like toys spilled from a box.

'Cheap, yes,' she said, 'but nothing goes this time of year except Christmas presents. We might make a do of it in the cottage shop.' The premises had been for sale so long they seemed to be sinking into the ground.

'Funny how buildings deteriorate once they're empty,' her husband was pleased to comment. She chose to ignore it.

The town, it seemed, perched chancily on the edge of things, had no place for a 'Party Planner'. Cakes and cider and home-brewed ales were comfortable entertainments, flashing lights, masks and paper hats, funny or foreign, were not.

'When they've got over the shock,' Sylvia explained to her family, 'it will inject new life. Wait and see!' She pictured for them, drifting across the valley, balloons with her name on.

'What will you be advertising?' Edward asked mildly.

'Hill Watch,' she was quick to reply.

'People certainly would.'

'You must admit some of my ideas have possibilities.'

Impatiently, she arrived first for the next meeting. The crowd was smaller than before.

'It's a preposterous idea,' Gerald laughed.

'But effective,' she cried.

'Wouldn't it frighten the sheep?'

'And frighten', she continued meaningfully, 'certain people who have settled up there.'

'There's no one up there.' He was reassuring.

'Oh yes, there are!'

He continued to address the meeting. 'We have posters with a message, not amounting to a threat, but a proposition.' After which twenty-two people arranged to meet in cars and on foot at a point known as Hill 1, later Hill 2, the following Sunday if fine for an investigatory walk.

'No sign of your wife then?' The policeman, in touch with the Weatherstones since the disappearance of Jemima, wife, mother and artist had become a nuisance. He had been forced to pack the boys off to London to a friend who lived near the zoo. The local community was thrilled and embarrassed. He was outraged. He didn't care if his wife came or went. He had ceased to be emotionally involved with her long ago. She was like the climate, would blow with the wind, warm in the sun, or, like rain, a bloody nuisance. He had made arrangements to go back to London himself, before Christmas if he could, if not, the day after. In one week he had become even more detached from the place, if that were possible.

'I have to let her go,' he confided to Sylvia. 'She has health problems, mental you know,' he added for good measure.

'I'm so sorry,' she had sympathised. 'Come here whenever you like.' He would really have to reassure the constabulary before her eccentricities could affect his career. On impulse he invited two friends to stay.

In that curtain of rain, like strands that tangled around her arms and legs, who could blame her, Jemima reasoned, for rushing with the sheep to another pasture, where a human being might find comfort in a house or at worst a barn or shed. Someone surely would take her in. She hated Gerald, pretended to like their open relationship, but in reality it made her insecure and denied her position. Now in extreme discomfort, she wanted revenge. She blamed herself for agreeing to come to such an uncivilised place. Then, a new situation presenting a new challenge.

'I'm so wet I can't worry any more,' she told the farmer and curled up in a chair. They were angels, giving her clothes and food and a bed, asking no questions. Her two phone calls went unanswered.

'I told you, I can't worry any more,' she assured them. 'I feel so safe at last I won't want to leave.'

'We do B & B,' they were encouraging her. It was perfect.

'Brilliant,' she said. 'Will you trust me? I have a cheque in the car but I don't know where it is. My husband is Gerald Weatherstone.'

They gave her food. The next day she went with the daughter of the house into the town on the pretext of arranging transport, giving herself time to think. No one could be expected to drive her hundreds of miles to consoling friends, all of who lived in cities. Her telephone call that morning, still unanswered, her position made her tearful. She was given another meal. Confidence renewed she bluffed it out one more night. 'I hate him,' she

55

told herself, 'and anyway I'm leaving.'

In this part of the land where everyone was related and business linked, a car was located going 'London' way. One look at the sexy driver and Jemima knew she was onto a good thing. With relief she got in the car, waving like a queen.

'Have you sent the Member of Parliament his bill?' the farmer's wife asked in her hearing. The farmer, a stubborn man told her, 'Bills went yesterday, next lot next week.' Jemima smiled and waved again, knowing they would add a bit on.

'No,' she said after a night in a motel and gave the car owner a wrong phone number. She didn't want to see him again. London was here, noisy, dirty, safe.

Her friends declared they knew she would be back and put her up in the studio. Lying on a familiar sofa with broken springs she adjusted the black cushions and let her eyes drift over each familiar object.

'Heaven,' she said alone in the empty room. Her companions had gone to a pub. There was a half-drunk bottle of wine on the table. She wanted nothing more than this easy paradise with people who argued and banged about and got on with their life expecting her to follow or go her way drifting in their timeless state which was neither day nor night. Hours later she had an unexpected desire to phone Gerald. She had ignored the answerphone before. Now she was ready. Pouring a quantity of wine into a glass, she took three large swigs and held her breath. The bleeps echoed and in the silence she waited. Indecision, which was not her usual style, held her back. She drank some more and spluttering down the line hoped it sounded right. 'Gerald,' she had started, perhaps with the hint of a party.

'Gerald, I'm sorry. I'm in Fulham with the usual lot. It's been hell but now I'm teaching, it'll be better. I'll write. Really sorry. Bye.' She finished the bottle and could have done with more. The country stay had been a nightmare of cold and rain and quarrelling. It was a bad time of year, a bad place. She had felt no call of the mountains and couldn't paint. The next day, finding a bottle of black nail varnish and certain items of clothing she went with a group to an art class the next evening and the following day at her old art college took a life-study session for nothing, referring to it as 'Work' in a letter. Long before her rambling account had been stamped and posted, news had reached Maesford.

Dear Elida,

I've so much to tell you I don't know where to start. I'm at Art School now. It's great.

I really really like it and should have done it ages ago. It's brilliant and – wait for it – there's a brilliant teacher here who comes from Maesford called Jemima Weatherstone. You must know her. Ask your parents.

Elida read on without enthusiasm. There was something disagreeable about another's success when one only knew failure. Despite this she experienced a little glow of pride at being the first with some news, of no interest to her but enough she guessed to startle other people.

'Mum,' she said, going up to the desk where Sylvia Bailey was working.

'Do you know Jemima Weatherstone?'

'Good God!' Sylvia gave her daughter for the only time in her life, her undivided attention.

'She's teaching at Maddy's Art School.'

'Good heavens!' Her mother shot through with such electrifying news, picked up a phone only pausing to include her daughter with a hug, finger poised over numbered digits.

Excitement had made her affectionate. 'Darling! She's been missing.'

'Oh!' Elida was good at pretending.

'She disappeared. Now you say she's turned up in London!' Tap, tap went digit after digit. Elida felt bound to sit in a chair and listen to the non-mystery.

'Gerald?' Sylvia's voice came out higher than her practiced recording tone. 'Did you know? We've just heard Jemima's working in London.'

'Oh, yes.' There was an imperceptible pause. A politician should know everything. His wife's method of communication was typical but he experienced disappointment.

'What a worry for you.'

'No really. She's always doing this. Maddening woman.'

'Even so,' Sylvia continued, 'we could all see you were concerned. And there was your family, and work, of course.'

'Look, I've friends here. Drop in for a drink. The usual arrangement, any time, we're here a lot and it's only down the road. About the one good thing in this place, you can drop in for a drink at any time without feeling embarrassed.'

'Yes, Gerald, I'm so glad for you.'

'Bloody woman.' Gerald put the phone down a little too quickly, knowing she wasn't and knowing she'd be around. The answerphone still held his wife's message.

Considered at a distance country life was interesting, country life had been fun. Uncomfortable as an experience, like a husband, Jemima opined, but, like a world in a soap opera, magnetic. She was impatient to know what would happen in the next episode. Information came occasionally from one of her students but she believed it to be exaggerated. Yet she herself had felt depressed and a victim of its raw climate, and could sympathise to some extent with a wayward society caught between past and present. It had an air of unreality where people performed in a dream. It was toytown. What were they doing up in the mountains, living wild? She guessed they were kids, drinking in the marshes, with handsome men, driving to secret places through the night. She felt a twinge of envy. Gerald was adequately entertained. Gossip she hardly bothered with, herself at the centre, but she was reminded that the same chaotic life went on in little pockets everywhere. She could not be silent for ever. Contact was irresistible.

'Any news from home?' she asked Madeline Chinthurst, known to the world as Maddy, like one who had made herself a star. The regular instalments of country life from the usual source had ceased, leaving Jemima distanced and shut out.

'You know what it is,' Maddy confided. 'You have to be there to know.'

'When are you going back?' Jemima asked pointedly.

'I dunno,' was all the answer she got from a girl with too many choices. She was getting old. She knew it the day she kicked that car driver out, bored and sick. After a good night with friends she was herself again, it didn't take much, and got Gerald to come down the next weekend. Soon it would be Christmas.

At certain times of the day smoke rose from the chimneys of the town and, looking down on the valley, smoke curled from all the cottage chimneys in reply like signals. The Vaughans had lit their fire and the Marchell family, Lynne, her elder sister Cherie and two brothers, were back together for regular family meals.

'I see your boyfriend's in trouble again.' Old man Marchell chuckled malevolently. If he could find fuel he would help to keep any fire going.

'I haven't got a boyfriend.' His daughter was ready for him.

'Oh yes? I thought you had plenty.'

'What's happened to Clifford?' Her sister had always been a jealous rival.

'You can have him. He's horrible.'

'Thanks. I've had that one and he's not.'

'He is. I know what you don't know then.'

'Ha, Ha!' The elder sister crowed in bad temper. 'Hark at her.' She continued to whisper something that no one heard and was prepared to go on.

'Better than the other one. Too old for you.' Lynne found all references to Aledd upsetting. She rose from the chair.

'Sit down, girl, and finish your dinner. Don't worry her!' Her mother thumped potatoes on the plates in silence. A cat mewed outside.

'I want to know why you don't like Clifford,' her sister sneered.

Lynne pushed back the food.

'Well, they'll get him – the other one – if he's not careful.' Father was taking control.

'Leave him alone. He's done nothing to you.' Her tears were rising.

'Oh, yes, he has. He nearly ruined my daughter.'

'What?' Lynne threw down her knife and fork.

'Nearly killed you.'

'He did nothing.' She screamed the last word. 'Nothing,' she

59

said again. 'Nothing.' Tears showed on her face. 'He's being victimised.' She flung herself from the room.

'We'll soon see!' Her father had been waiting for the right time to release the fury that had been growing in him as the pace of local interest quickened and became the gossip of street corners. 'We'll see!' As his anger smouldered, the words choked him.

'Now, this time! Yeah, this time. You...'

'Don't upset her, George. It's been bad for her but she's better.'

'Ahh!' her father growled like a dog.

'Not better,' her brother took it up. 'She's always crying.'

'Leave her be!'

'He beat her up.' There were few secrets that were not made public here.

'Which one?'

'The other one!'

'Oh?'

Sitting in her bedroom, Lynne thought of Aledd. She imagined him sitting alone or with his parents in the farmhouse across the marsh. She hoped there was no one else in his life, aware people still mentioned his name. She knew girls from the town went to his coffee room but even jealousy would not let her speak to him. It was easy to walk past the place, perhaps tomorrow it might happen, he would come out and she could acknowledge him in some way. She would not go in.

Aledd lit a fire. He was not at the farm. In his mountain hideout, the wind blew across the floor and lifted fragments of leaf that hung in the air before drifting into the corners of the room. He watched them catch in the smoke that twisted curiously around before being sucked up into the chimney to escape in the sky. A plume of smoke bent by the wind betrayed his presence. He did not stay long but used an hour or so of his time to free himself of troubles, light a fire, plan alterations to make this a permanent residence. He imagined a house or farm. In the spring he might improve the pool outside that was just a depression in the rock, a dip pool for cattle, construct a fence, a lean-to for the van. One feature, a tree spread sideways to protect the yard, rough ground where slate and stones were randomly set. Soon he left for the valley before he was missed, before anyone knew. No one must know.

Meetings for Hill Watch slowed to half speed. With Christmas approaching, once a fortnight was all anyone could manage. The mountains were abandoned to the elements, sheep brought down to more sheltered pastures, and small wild horses, brown, dun and shades of grey, disappeared into the low clouds before heading for the scrub trees for shelter when the wind raced. In back rooms and halls or people's kitchens carols were being rehearsed for the great celebration. Anyone who could hum was expected to sing. With a shortage of pianists mothers brought out shy daughters, and fathers given a stiff drink were persuaded to learn a tune or a chord or two. Finding his congregation reduced by these exercises, the vicar ordered the piano to be tuned in the older pub and orchestrated a mighty evening of song plus rehearsal.

'Is it a dry run, Vicar?'

'No,' said the vicar, a practiced man, referring to the scriptures.

The usual lessons and carols were heard in the town church, the church in the marsh, and the chapel in the foothills, screened from view. These celebrations could not hold a candle to The Black Ox whose mixed assembly, fortissimo in the stunning heat of the bar, drank beer to cool their throats.

Sylvia Bailey had sent her Christmas invitations so far in advance that no one had bothered to answer. 'And neither can one decently refuse,' whispered a critic.

Aledd practised the chapel organ late into the night. Never perfect, he was much in demand both as pianist and guitar player when he would strum three chords, unembarrassed by his limitations. Sometimes he heard footsteps approach and pass the chapel door. He took no notice, aware the police had extended their beat. These were the night sounds that mixed with owls and bats, and winds shifting the slates and putting pressure on old timbers. When footsteps approached, he felt neither fear nor guilt. He guessed it was the policeman, and was most certain of this when a torch flashed. He continued with the hymn he was playing, content that he was being protected.

One night, when he was restless, he went in the van and then on foot as far as the old hill plantation. In the past, a helicopter circled the area exposing a walker to such scrutiny that instinct would make him take cover. This time it was near dark but with partial light he found his way. With an Indian stealth, he walked in shadows by trees and close to outcrops of rock instead of striding across open ground. It was his habit, walking rabbit runs and sitting under scrub bushes, to watch small creatures before their time of rest. He was wholly at peace here, noting a similar peace in the animal life that was all around. At length he got up, remembering what he had come for. He searched bent to the earth to discover the feathered grasses that would enhance his present collection. If he found nothing today there would be more for tomorrow. He would never strip a crop bare. He straightened again looking up at the sky still glowing with light, and felt eyes upon him, strange eyes in the empty hill. He had made sure there was no one and had not thought about it until this tingling moment of shock.

'You are a night bird like me,' said the eyes.

He despised torches. Most of the time he walked in the dark. It was more fun. Crossing home from the chapel he knew every hazard. Here it was the same. The wider the territory the more the excitement. He brushed around a hedge and a figure emerged from the trees.

'Well now!' He recognised the voice before the torch shone in his face.

He continued, taking a similar torch from his pocket and, like a flare, held it at the policeman's head.

'Are you trying to scare me?'

The policeman laughed.

It was Aledd who was to initiate the next conversation. 'Are you going to arrest me?' He was determined to keep control.

The policeman laughed again. It was a genuine laugh, recognised as a greeting to a friend.

'Don't play games with me, Clive. Are you arresting me?'

'Not this time.' The voice was authoritative. 'I'm not playing games. You go around a lot in the dark.'

'So do you.'

'It's my job.'

'And this is home ground,' Aledd replied. 'It's great, with strangers taking over. Good to have the mountains to myself, night is best!'

'So I see!'

'I work late. During the day the place is overrun with them.'

'This far?'

'Not this far.' Aledd laughed this time. 'Some areas are tourist attractions but some places they'll never know.'

'You know them then?'

'Of course I do!' He was going to add, 'And so do you,' but stopped, and thought why was he being followed? They were walking together in an open space, two torches lighting two pairs of feet.

'These places you know.'

Aledd thought, Does he mean my place in the plain?

The policeman was continuing, '...Where we raided the drug gang.'

'I remember the helicopters.' It seemed so long ago, Aledd felt able to show an interest in history. He said aloud, 'A long time ago, a few years.' They had walked to a small slatted bridge like a pile of stones over glinting water.

'Well, they're back.' The voice carried a threat or a warning, he did not know which.

'No!' said Aledd, and, forced to go on, 'How can you be sure?'

'We've seen them.'

'Oh?' He had condemned himself, thinking too slow. Now he was faced with some admission and chose a lesser failing, was considered a fault.

'I go out at night.'

'Where exactly?'

'I go somewhere private. The shepherd's hut, the ruin near the Red Hill. I've fixed it up. That's all right, isn't it?'

'I should think so. I couldn't say.'

'I've been doing it for a long time.' He hoped he was leading the policeman to safer ground. 'The places don't belong to anyone, do they?'

'I couldn't say.' Aledd felt threatened and could only keep his nerve by talking. 'Since we lost the cottage – my girlfriend and I – I've had nowhere that's mine.'

'You live at home, don't you?'

'That's not private, not like the cottage was.' He was going to say, 'Why did they turn me out?' But he needed to back down. He needed anonymity. He had always been the accused.

'Hard on you but there were reasons. The place is up for sale now. Maybe they'll rebuild it.'

'I don't go there now.'

'There's another place.'

'What other place?'

'The old plantation fields. You go there?'

'No. Yeah. Well. I go all over.' As they continued to walk, 'Hills are free like me.'

'Not much longer if you are breaking the law. You will lose more than your house.'

'Who says I'm breaking the law?'

'There's talk!'

'I've committed no crime.'

'That's not what they say. There are young people at risk, young girls. You've been seen with them.'

'Never.'

'They talk to you.'

'Oh yes they do. I let them. Do you want to know just what I tell them? Leave some things alone. They come for alcohol. I sell them coffee! Do they tell you that?' He was angry now.

'I'm glad to hear it. Drugs? Okay boy!'

'Don't call me boy. I was at school with you, remember?'

'Okay, I said.'

'Don't hound me.'

'Be careful, Aledd. I'm on your side.' Was he offering friendship?

'Are you on my side? You watched them take my job away! Home! Girl! Now it's the stone place! I suppose that's what you are here for. The hills are mine, the cabin is mine, this land is mine as much as anyone. This land is free, free! Not you, not anyone can change that.'

64

'I can take your freedom. Don't forget it.'

'Lock me up, then!' Suddenly, he didn't care any more.

'Must do my job. I was asked to question you and I have. I chose to do it here in the open, on neutral ground. I could have had you down at the station but I didn't.'

Aledd felt the heat leave his face. They were hidden by the night, black shapes in a field. His anger, invisible, hung in the air. Voice answering voice had ceased. Only their footfalls could be heard brushing the grass. They stood now.

'Okay, I understand.'

The flare of a match lit a face and died to leave the small red glow of a cigarette. The red glow was fixed in space, alive.

'Want one?'

The red spot was fading away, with the voice. He thought it said, 'I think we understand each other. I hope so for your sake.' The sound was muffled.

He wanted to stay out there in the hills but he must work tomorrow. Yes, he must work. The work was bringing him money. With money he could do anything. He felt elated, the battle won. Instead of going home he went to the chapel. By the orange light he tried to play a carol. He liked the idea of a guiding star, 'Did the guiding star behold', he played. But it was too late. There were no stars. He went home. The next day disturbed by the events that had pursued him through the night the sound stayed in his head of the husky moan of the chapel organ and the words of a hymn.

He decided to give up his night excursions and, this time, go to the chapel in the afternoon. Encouraged by the sunshine, he set out as soon as he could and found the door unlocked as usual. Added warmth gave the building a different air. Gone were the shadows from the low electric light. In their place, rays full of stars, formed by particles of dust, stretched from the windows to the floor, warmed the seat as he sat at the old harmonium, and danced on his hand as he played. He started at the beginning of the book. Played the first carol but went on to do it again. It gave him a special satisfaction to know that he could at least play one piece well for the Christmas service. He started on another, awkwardly. Runs of notes jerked under his fingers, wooden after mixing and lifting pounds of cement and stone. With the thought of his shepherd's hut, he slipped for a moment into dreaming when fear shot deep in his chest, left him helpless, his hands on the keys. A cloud had covered the sun. He looked up at the dark form of the vicar.

'I've startled you. That's too bad. I was trying not to interrupt and hoped you wouldn't notice me. It's sounding quite good. What a talented chap you are. I'm grateful for your time. You seem to be everywhere as far as I can see.' He laughed to himself at an idea that was not so much amusing as curious.

'I did want to speak to you.' The tone was sympathetic but Aledd heard a warning. He stiffened. Inhaling the dry air, he prepared himself for a repetition of the night before. He was to be examined again. He was waiting, his eyes down. Slowly he folded his arms. His hands clutched his sides.

'I don't mean to worry you. I am the one who is worried. I know you are a hard-working sincere person. There is so much friction. This is my worry. I must explain. There are tensions in the town. Everyone has them. I am ignorant of the cause of many. You will know more, of course, because you are part of the place and know everyone in a personal way. I am really trying to enlist your help. Can you help me, I wonder? I know you have had your problems. I would like to think you would feel free to come to me. Perhaps, but I doubt it. You won't. You are a different generation and vicars you think ignore the world in favour of spiritual things. But how's that girlfriend of yours? Or perhaps you have split up. Dumped? Dumped do you call it?'

For the first time in days, Aledd could smile. 'No.' Instead of threatening, the vicar had cheered him up. They were both smiling. The whole subject sounded funny from a vicar in chapel. 'At one time, I thought she had dumped me. We're sort of friends.'

'That's good. That's all right then.' Having sat down abruptly he got up to make a final point. 'Can we try, you and I, and the rest of the community, to come together to resolve our differences. We are all to blame. We bring things on ourselves. There's no doubt of that.' He was going but as an afterthought.

'You are not mixed up with the hill drug dealers are you? I

hope you are not. I have heard you are. Your life has been troubled and this could destroy you. I am not passing judgment but I believe this will do untold damage. There are those looking to you for a lead.'

He hurried out. 'It's the opposite…' Aledd started to say, but he had gone. Aledd was alone. The afternoon's peace would not come back again and he was not able to continue.

There was one thing on his mind that started to grow, as a hint becomes a suggestion. So casually mentioned it was not a statement of fact, that at first he dismissed it as fanciful. Today with time to spare he gave it some thought. At the right time of year a man could quickly produce a crop of something, harvest it and vanish, providing the area was remote enough, away from unmarked tracks. It was a daring idea, been tried before and aborted. He paused for a while, good sense pointing to one more mistake. He had made many mistakes – bad decisions not realised until too late, action, result, repentance. Would this be different? To clear his mind, he would drive, if there was petrol enough, somewhere new. He might visit the mountains where the air was light. As was his habit, he drove part of the way and then continued on foot. Soon he found freedom again and his old optimistic self. He looked for two things, wheel tracks off the grazing routes, some form of marker on ground cleared close from bracken baling. As usual the black rolls stood line after line, huge wheels ready for winter beds when they would disappear leaving the land strangely bare. He moved on scanning the ground. He knew what he was looking for, those shy little plants, forbidden, exciting. He was a man for whom both time and events were adjustable. Some things seemed so long ago they had vanished, had never existed. In the same way, when Christmas was near he saw spring in the turf and seedlings before they started to grow. Spring was near him now and behind it summer when the bracken would rise and shield the plot on which he stood like a dark forest. He looked for a change in the natural order of things, a man's hand perhaps. At the end of the day he wasn't sure.

'Can we seat sixteen without a squash?' Sylvia Bailey liked

formality.

'Don't worry, at least two will cancel. The Jeromes are always away.' It would please Edward if they were. He was getting too involved. Ann was on his mind, and he suffered from indigestion when he was nervous. 'The vicar?' he went on.

'Yes.'

'Has Weatherstone's bohemian wife come back yet?'

'No, but she will. Please leave the guest list to me. Make a seating plan if it will amuse you.'

'You only change it.'

'Yes, that's the fun.'

He picked up a pen but he had forgotten the name of the vicar's wife, and settled to the crossword.

'I'm going out.'

'Right.' He was aware he lived in a busy household but there was never anyone around. The place, empty of human life reverberated with energy that made the curtains sway. The crossword was a difficult one. He made coffee. The desk would be full of lists from now on, food, presents, the tree. Something evergreen would be cut down from the garden, it being impossible to buy anything of suitable size. It would be placed in a dustbin and strapped at all points to banister rails. Up to the ceiling it would go, lights flickering. The floor areas being in darkness, walking was a hazard. Sylvia would advise guests to memorise the layout as soon as possible, each year it was the same. Soon meals would be served on trays leaving the dining room free for his wife to exercise her wilder decorative notions. The table would look elegant, he knew. Flowers would be kept to a minimum. No chance of hiding from Ann's dark eyes. That had been the trouble in the first place. Let Sylvia ogle Gerald, he liked quietly to eat.

His wife's schemes were impossible to control. He saw, the day she sprayed the flowers gold, there was something uncultivated in her energies, while Ann Jerome's displeasure grew and died under lowered lids. Her burning eyes, he thought and with an effort thought of something else. When they sat down, thirteen, Sylvia made a speech. Anyone who didn't like it could sit out and be Judas. There was a stunned silence. As a diversion the vicar said grace, during which people studied the plates of smoked salmon – except Sylvia and Edward whose plates were empty. 'Amen,' said Edward to the plate and for another diversion poured the wine. His wife sat in a trance.

'Perhaps you have a cat?' said the vicar's wife.

Indeed they had a cat of singularly ugly mien banished to the garden. It must have slipped into the two most inviting chairs, their arm rests freeing them from the table.

'I hope he hasn't licked mine!' Heads turned. It was Rosemary, wretched girl. 'It looks disturbed,' she continued, as one pleased to criticise.

'A fiasco,' called Sylvia through the hatch.

'Give it to me.' Someone was sympathetic. 'Sylvia's disturbed enough.'

'We thought you were both on a diet!' They were still offering solutions, but plates were whisked away and peeled grapes appeared gold as decorations, tumbled in glass dishes surprised or squashed like the guests according to their natures.

'A pity,' Edward murmured liking smoked salmon.

'Always prepared,' said his wife pouring salad dressing.

'This is an un-Christmas party,' Edward went on. His wife shot him a glance. He smiled. He had certainly changed since they had moved here. Pheasants, carefully carved and remoulded, were wafted in, their feathers quivering in tufts where once were tails.

'Guess who's having the parson's nose?' Everyone knew Jemima was back.

'She'll never change,' Sylvia said to Gerald, 'but then you're used to it.'

'Do you get poachers?' he returned, well able to control Sylvia.

'Not since that awful man.'

'Don't, Mummy?' Elida had to shout across the table.

'What man?' Jemima as usual had started on her dinner partner's wine, her husband noted.

'We've lived in a nightmare here.' Sylvia was telling her tale. 'An ex-employee. He turned out to be the cause of the trouble. I think he did it purposely.'

'Really? In what way?' Someone at the end of the table was

leading her on.

'He redecorated the whole house while we were away.'

'Shop,' corrected Edward.

'How fascinating. Did you like it?'

'Like it?' Sylvia's voice crackled with suppressed fire. 'Huh,' she went on with the story. 'Everything was missing. I think he stole. We couldn't find our most basic equipment. He was a thief given a free hand.'

'Sylvia, be careful. You have no proof.'

'The police searched his house.'

'But they didn't find anything.'

'Sells drugs and seduces young girls, what more is there?'

'Sylvia, please.' She recognised the note of despair that signalled defeat.

The vicar spoke. 'Well,' he started. They waited for a sermon. 'I should like some more peas.'

'Help the vicar, someone.'

'I can see I have stayed away too long.' Sitting at an angle Jemima contrived to switch glasses with her husband who was watching the progress of the bowl of peas.

Observed, she said as an apology, 'He never likes white wine,' and she drank in the silence. 'Well,' she said again, 'this man – he works at a pub, doesn't he? I hear he's quite attractive.'

'Jemima, this is not a festive conversation.' Her husband attempted to control her.

'Oh, yes it is!' He had failed. 'Let's have some more of this lovely stuff.' She rattled the base of the glass on the table.

'Jemima behave yourself. This is not the King's Road.'

'Of course. Edward, wine!' Sylvia, never without a motive encouraged her.

Edward rose. 'Red or white?'

'Both! Either.' Jemima and her husband spoke in unison.

Sylvia was off. 'We have the most amazing society – village and town, primitive country mixed up with a civilised way of life. I hardly like Elida to go about alone.'

'Mummy, it's all in your mind.'

'It's not, my dear. Men live rough in the hills. The pheasant is not poached, you will be glad to hear. It's probably one of the few that's left. It's quite easy to live free.'

'Sherwood Forest,' a man's voice.

'Thousands of sheep roam the place. Pheasants, rabbits, pigeons and all that marijuana. Edward, don't glare at me. It's common knowledge and something should be done.'

'We have set up a local association to deal with just such eventualities.' Gerald Weatherstone leaned back, fingers together pitched as a church roof, assuming his chairman's position.

'I don't think.' The vicar leaned forward. They waited for the address. 'I don't think...' He favoured little repeats. 'I don't think...' the third time accompanied by a light laugh, 'we need concern ourselves now. Things will be under control. The police have it in hand.'

'What a lot. They are all in with the criminals.'

'Sylvia, this is preposterous. There are no criminals, as you call them, and the police are not corrupt. You breed discontent and fear with such a conversation. This is supposed to be Christmas and this subject is not Christmas fare.'

'This is an un-Christmas party, didn't I say? And as such this is a good time to have it out.' Sylvia was extremely excited. 'Well, Ben, as a churchman, support us. A girl in the village was raped. I hear the gossip.'

'It is gossip.' Edward's confidence was back.

'Mummy, it's not fair, is it, Maddy?' Maddy beamed, thrilled. 'Maddy, you know Aledd, too. He's nice. Everyone is kind and helpful.'

'Elida and you, Maddy, listen to me.' Sylvia sounded threatening. 'I forbid you to have conversations or anything to do with village men. Do you hear me? I am responsible for you, Maddy, while you are here. And Elida, I'm shocked. Where do you meet these people? Vicar – er – Ben, I'm sorry if this is an unsuitable time, but I'm horrified and what is more, scared. My daughter is in danger. She may not be an adventurous girl but she is vulnerable. And you, Maddy, are too high-spirited and fun loving. You will get yourself into trouble. Nobody has been murdered yet, but it will happen.'

'Sylvia, my dear.' The vicar spoke low, paternal. 'You must not disturb yourself unduly. This is all hearsay.'

'Disturbed, I have been disturbed ever since we came here. This is a horrible place. I'm sorry everyone – Edward, wine – I'm unburdening myself. It's unforgivable at a party.'

'Sylvia, this is not a horrible place.' Ann Jerome's voice had more than it's usual drawl.

'You may think so, Ann. You're always away.' She suspected Ann of a double life.

Ann answered with a laugh which quietly said, 'No.'

Jemima was so entertained and she said, to keep the storm rolling, 'Elida, I've a wonderful idea. Why don't you and I and Maddy – they'll be safe with me Sylvia – go to that pub, what's it called? – The Black Ox.'

'I forbid it.' Sylvia in frenzy slapped the table. 'I absolutely forbid it. Jemima please keep out of this. You know nothing of things here and apparently think this is Chelsea.'

'Sylvia,' Edward warned.

'Sylvia,' Gerald rebuked, playfully, 'my wife is happy-go-lucky. It's her artistic temperament, she tells me, always the child, impetuous not irresponsible. However, Jemima, this is not a good idea. I hope the girls will come over, tomorrow, if you like, or soon, and we'll have a sailing party.'

'A sailing party?' Jemima exploded, 'How bizarre. Drive a hundred miles and get wet. My idea is much better. I'll take the girls on a…' – she avoided 'pub crawl' – 'casual lunch somewhere and they can show me the district.'

'You have never shown any interest in the district – as you call it – the last time you got washed down a mountain and ran away!' Gerald was callous in this mood.

'Rubbish. I was driven away by your obsession with the countryside. I got a lift to London. It was a chance in a million that anyone would offer me a lift in an isolated farm. I took it. You should check your answerphone or have a fax like everyone else.'

'I'm sorry my wife drinks so much. Forgive her, Sylvia. Jemima shut up. Don't quarrel with me now. We'll take the girls on a friend's boat, and their mother too.'

'Oh.' Sylvia was placated, but not Jemima.

'I'm going back to London if you insist on organising me.'

'I'm not organising you, but you can forget educating the young. Apologies everyone.' Gerald sounded final.

'During our travels – Sylvia is quite right – we are not good participants locally, I'm afraid but it's the way we like it – during our travels.' John Jerome had successfully cooled the temperature of the room. They watched in surprise as he spoke for the first time. 'We found some wonderful wines. I'm not a wine snob, before somebody says I am, but a change is good for us all. They are not as good as these,' he touched his glass, 'but good enough. Why don't you all come to our place? You know where we are.'

'Where?' Jemima looked like having her best Christmas.

'Chorley's, on a level here but on the other road facing south. I was going to suggest we repeat this fine occasion, before Christmas, of course, before we leave.'

'Goody.' Jemima was deciding for them all.

'Not if you repeat this performance,' her husband muttered.

The Jeromes invitation damped Sylvia's rage but it was in danger of breaking out again. At the words 'fine occasion', Edward glanced at Ann, fearing irony but she wore her blank look. He checked the faces of his guests in turn and focused on 'my best friend Rosemary'. For his wife, a name needed qualifying. Rosemary, a good-looking woman but whose colourless hair had now lost itself with her face took her cue.

'It would be fun if we could do it in turn. I could be next with Vanessa.' Vanessa murmured something. There was a pause. The fire had gone out, and with it the warmth. No sound but the click of a knife on a plate and another echoing round the table as if responding to a signal. Muted from the effort of controlling a quarrel they were ready for home.

'Brulee?' Sylvia recovered first. 'Or jelly or cheese?' With a sigh her husband went in search of brandy.

'I dunno, I rather fancy some whisky.' Jemima's voice was one level above a whisper. 'If you say one more thing,' her husband hissed, but it was the excuse that Edward needed. He moved a chair by her side and sat on it.

'What a good idea. You and I, both.'

Gerald in need of exercise moved in masterly style across the room.

73

'Cigar?' Sylvia chimed in her brightest voice.

The vicar rose next. 'Seeing that we're changing round…' he descended on his hostess, who smiled appealingly at John Jerome who came back with his party offer.

'Next week then at Chorley's!'

'Tomorrow's morning service…' The vicar's words lay heavily on Sylvia.

'Yes, I suppose so.' Her head was splitting.

'Elida, should you be drinking whisky? It's not a good mixture.'

The evening was taking a new turn. The table looked a shambles. People relaxing, were now getting drunk. She wondered if her face was as red as Vanessa's. Joy Tooley – Sylvia never understood why Edward never knew names – was building a castle with mint wafers. Red wine had spilled like a map on the cloth.

'Excuse me…' but before she could get up, her husband signalled her to leave it.

'Sorry, Mrs Bailey. I think it was me. Sorry!' Maddy's face swam before her, matching the wine.

She had to go out. Walking unsteadily to the kitchen and the company of her clean, cool, time-saving machines, she held ice to her wrists and the back of her neck. In the other room only the Jeromes remained unmoved and smiled enigmatically at each other. Sylvia knew she must not absent herself for long. The disgrace of her disintegrating dinner party would become common gossip. The Jeromes entertaining them with dubious wines was turning the knife in the wound. Banishing all these foolish thoughts with a shake of her head she stepped briskly back to rescue the vicar to whom she knew she had been rude.

'Coffee?' she cried a little shrilly.

The vicar had vanished. As she sat once more she thought she saw him with her daughter behind a potted plant.

'My dear, we're off.'

'Gerald, so soon and before coffee?'

'Yes, yes, we must.' Was he laughing? 'It's been hilarious, but I must do something with Jemima. I'm sick of her performances, but she's having them in stitches so I'll get her away while she's ahead.'

'We'll take some coffee into the hall.'

'Right.'

'Coffee in the hall everyone.'

'Out before we disgrace ourselves.' Vanessa's man who no one knew looked tired.

'Good.'

'Marvellous.'

'Out everyone,' and they were gone or going like an army bearing trophies. Joy carrying the flowers from the table, presumably for the church as the vicar had some too. Maddy held a tea towel to her face, the outcome of the wine and whisky she feared.

'We've never enjoyed anything more!' Her two women friends kissed her. What had happened while she was in the kitchen? Only the Jeromes were in the dining room. She went back to placate them and salvage some of her dignity.

'Rather a rabble, I'm afraid,' she said, sitting down, 'shall we go in the other room?'

'No, my dear, it's late. You have entertained us well and we enjoyed the lively exchange.'

Sylvia looking for euphemisms found one. 'Unseemly row,' she concluded. 'I'm sorry.'

'Why should you be? We understand.' United in good form, they spoke for each other, no chink in the armour, enviable. She in contrast, seen off-guard, had revealed herself in all her weakness and ignorance. Goaded by silly people she had failed socially. Edward was no help. Sometimes he seemed to be taking sides against her. Abandoning pride she made a final effort.

'I do appreciate your friendship.'

'Well, my dear, you'll come to us next week.' And they went.

Even their exits were high form, a kiss, a little smile and no looking back. She countered by closing the door, not waiting for them to disappear. Why should she? They would never turn and wave. She had ceased to exist once they faced the other way. Stuck up, she thought then blamed herself again for not thanking little Karen in the kitchen.

Karen! She had forgotten to pay her. Choosing a style between grand and familiar, she sat as one in delicate health, a hand to her head. Karen was smoking and finishing someone's wine. She seemed to be enjoying it.

'That's right. Finish it up.'

'Thanks, Mrs Bailey.' Her smile was reassuring. Sylvia felt the atmosphere change. A nice girl, she thought sitting opposite her as she moved through the chairs and tables and ate cheese and a grape.

'Do you ever see anything of Lynne? Lynne Marchell.'

'Yes, she's all right.'

Learning nothing she probed deeper. 'Not getting married?' Despite the pause she was confident. 'I suppose they've broken up.'

'Who?'

'You know. What's his name.'

'Aledd, you mean?' The sound of the name upset her again but she was determined to go on. 'Yes,' and she waited for several seconds before another attempt. 'I think she was ill or something.'

'Yes. They split up but I think they're back together now.'

This was not what she wanted to hear. Whatever might be said to help her cause it was not this. Discomforted she walked away calling from the hall, 'I'll get your money.'

She didn't know why the Lynne girl upset her so much, but the idea of a man in a pub attracting her daughter, who frequented the coffee lounge, was cause for concern. And the idea of Elida hanging round a bar with the disagreeable name of 'The Black Ox' conjured up a revolting picture of degeneracy in a subculture that she could only half imagine but had come to haunt her. Tomorrow she would walk down the town just to see what was happening. She would pass by, stepping close to the windows which came down low to the street. She might catch sight of her daughter and Maddy, her unruly friend. She would not go in, but if necessary ban Maddy from the house. She had enough on her to make a good case including drinking and consorting with a shepherd who was bound to behave as freely as in any myth and legend. She had decided, now she had definitely decided to go down the town, to investigate.

It seemed Lynne was of the same mind. Once she had been

happy, long ago, in the days of the old shop. Aledd was the subject of comment but still, she supposed, her friend. Then there was Christmas. She might lose him and be alone when the entire world was coupled. A sort of fear drove her out in new clothes. She got to the corner near the window before the sign of 'The Black Ox'. Walking past it was difficult to see in. She felt stupid standing on the doorstep. She felt awkward going in but was determined to ask after Aledd and buy something. He was standing before her. Once she thought of him as an attractive man. Today he was beautiful. His eyes, grey as the hill, changed in the bright light from the window to blue and all the colours of the newly painted room filtered onto his hair and face.

'I thought you would never come,' he said and leant forward to kiss her, but remembered. He remembered something that stopped him. Or was it they were not alone. He put a hand on her shoulder. He waited a second. She did not flinch.

'I miss you,' she said simply.

His smile came back. 'I'd better get you something. You can't just stand there, come into the coffee bar.'

'I heard about it,' she said.

There were just tables and chairs and cloths. Three red check cloths were enough. She remembered herself a year ago. A year ago when she was young. She remembered again being young and happy. They had taken the things from the shop out on the pavement in the sun. She made cakes and he had worn an apron; red, she thought. She loved him and he would kiss her leaning across a table and, later, when she walked beside him in the green valley with the hills at the back. She felt her eyes fill with tears.

'Can I kiss you?' he said like a boy. She nodded and cried. He kissed her as he used to across the table. It was as if they had gone back again and were happy. She sobbed. He took her silently through the room. In the window he sat her down and made her coffee.

When later she spoke she said, 'You should be wearing a red apron.'

He stood beside her and ran his fingers through her hair, combing it back as he remembered it.

'I've cut it.'

77

'I know.' He went on, the fingers of one hand slowly parting strands of her hair. 'Don't cry any more,' he said sternly.

She stopped crying and sat dry-eyed only aware of the movement of his hand. When someone entered the side bar he left her for a while and she remained quietly drinking coffee, stirring in sugar from a packet, no tremble of excitement nor fear. There was peace all around and inside her stillness she had not experienced before. There were voices in the next room but she stayed for a while then rose to her feet and slowly, steadily, crossed through to the busy bar and smiled as she left. Turning she kissed the air in front of four people she didn't know. She felt him behind her, heard him say he was sorry he had neglected her. She laughed and went out into the bright street.

Aledd strode through the week. He felt strong. When Sylvia Bailey stared at him through the window where he worked, he stared back. In that brief moment he was not sure if he saw hatred or something contrary in her look. He knew she held his eyes with hers. He experienced a feeling of amusement that a middle-aged woman, smart and good looking, should look at him, the barman at The Black Ox, in such a way, in such a meaning way. She went on down the road. He went on through the day. He walked home, then took the van and drove like the wind to the mountains.

It grew darker. As the road rose to 1500 feet, it shone black with rain and reflected gold in the headlamps. The rear wheels floundered in the turf and off the other side and back again. He didn't care where he went. He had some idea of the direction he would take once he left the van. It was an inadequate vehicle for the mountain. The wheels spun. He remembered the tyres were bad, but refused to let anything lower his spirits. He had pretended he could fly like a bird but his uncertain progress caused him to slow down and stop. He continued on foot, upwards by a crumbling wall to the remains of a stone bridge covered with weed. There were beautiful stones here, and slate and rock to make his place complete. As usual the air hung with moisture but in the protective silence he sensed movement behind or below him and stood still. There were people. He thought he heard voices, the sound of an engine and voices again. Taking a deep breath, he called. The silence was thick around him. To make sure he was in sole possession of the hill he called again.

His voice echoed, 'Hello there!'

It was just an echo. He breathed steam that blew back in his face. His heart raced, he had not been mistaken. He called again, embarrassed, shouting into space.

'Hello,' he called for the third time, and waited.

There had been someone there – he felt their presence – but now he was equally sure they had moved away, disappearing down the path he had so recently used to reach his private domain. He was on the highest point of a hill behind which, in the gap, were the twin hills, that sat like upturned pudding basins. The ruined shack lay hidden, protected from the elements, his, he had found it and with his hands made it his own. Low stone walls and channels of water crossed the plains, once good pasture overcropped, deserted except for a few ewes. No one came here. It was too exposed. On very hot days the water pools warmed and dried, although there was always a wind mysteriously cold. His first thought was to track the intruders, the second, to check his stone house. He had tamed it and eased it into shape and the idea that someone might enter it and disturb it in some way shocked him. He went onto the other side of the hill and looked across, studied it for a while.

An arch and the remains of a door stood guard, its threatening weight of stone menacing to the stranger in what light remained. He returned, his steps in the dark so slow there seemed no movement at all. As he approached, no one, he argued, would willingly enter that dark cave, no one except himself. Inside it was darker than shadows. It was fanciful of him to imagine it had been occupied. He walked slowly back by the wall and ditch, a mile down to the van.

He was convinced that someone had either sought him out, or was trying to get away from him. Once in the van, the lights bobbed along, turning the wet road surface from yellow to orange. The battery was down. At a junction once the main route to the village, he stopped, turned off the headlamps and revved up the engine.

'Waiting for someone?' The voice sent pins and needles down

his arms. He stared into the night. Out of the blackness a patrol car took shape. He might have hit it. Still in a state of shock, he was grateful for a familiar face above the torch beam.

'No. I was tracking someone from the hill. They came down here, I think.'

'I don't advise you to be in the hills this time of day.'

'Why not? I know them.' As an afterthought, he added, 'Like you.'

'Well you don't want to be around up there. There are undesirable people about.'

'You're joking! Who's around? Only the shepherd.'

'Having trouble with your lights?'

'It's the battery.'

'Better get it fixed. I don't want to nick you for a traffic offence.'

'I don't want you to nick me for anything. I'm a law-abiding citizen.' There was such a silence that Aledd made the point again. 'A law-abiding citizen.'

'I hope so.'

'You know so. Come on Clive, who's side are you on?' At school they had fought and ended friends twenty years ago. 'You know me,' he went on. 'You never know newcomers. You can go to their meetings and rely on them to stick together. I've seen some, remember? If you want to know, ask me. I know.'

'Mebbe.'

'Don't you think so?'

'Mebbe.'

'Well, I can't stop. Made it up with Lynne and I don't want to spoil it.'

'That's so?'

'Yep.'

'How is she?'

'Brilliant.'

'Drive carefully.'

Aledd revved hard, putting up the lights and shot off before they let him down. Had he made a good case for himself? His police friend spoke to him like a stranger. He regained some of his high spirits as the street lamps brought the town nearer. He felt like talking to people, food and drink. The pub was waiting for him.

'Just a quick pint,' said the vicar, 'and a word with you.'

When people asked for 'a word', he felt they were pointing a gun at his head, but the vicar smiled and looked at his watch.

'Oh, the time! The meeting! Still, we're having the usual services in the church.' He indicated the town stretching above them, 'And the little chapel for the old residents with the Rev. Hughes, I mean real local people you know. You will play there won't you, as we're without our usual organist? Or perhaps you can think of someone else?' Aledd couldn't. 'Or my wife might do it.'

'Yes,' said Aledd, stating a preference.

'Then there's the other idea. Church and chapel in the pub. You could do refreshments.'

'Yes.' For the first time he began to warm to the festive season.

'The only thing is, the other pub where you used to work are rather keen. Nothing is simple, but these differences, once resolved make for a better community, I always say, so we must resolve them.'

'What do you want me to do about it?' Aledd was in the mood to lead.

'I don't know yet.' The vicar was not making decisions today. 'However you are such a helpful member of the old town,' he stressed 'old town', 'I shall put your case,' and, remembering discord, 'I shall put my case for having it here.'

He bustled out, spoke to four people and was late. He liked to be late but this was lax. Late he could avoid the preamble, but, given time, affairs could run ahead in a direction he, for one, did not wish to go. 'Wretched Sylvia Bailey,' he sighed, and, 'wretched Gerald Weatherstone for joining her.' He stumped on up the hill with no time to look back at the mountains, which always returned him to sanity. His thoughts were now on choir practice which would have to be brief again. He must leave early, but his affection for the place was so strong he minded leaving. In times of stress, when he considered escape, faith brought him back, a faith in people as universal as any inner force, but overriding this was a vision of Sylvia's private army. He didn't know what it was about that woman, but she would disturb Utopia.

When he arrived five years ago the town was a backwater. Many had left for a better life. Few returned but there were still some, one or two scattered like wild flowers that clung to their natural soil. Mocked by the adventurous, they were the strongest he was convinced and his job was to give them support. Here was a place of countless resources. He was supporting them in their absence. His head, that minutes earlier had been left in The Black Ox while his legs took him up the hill, given a dash of air, caught up with him at last and in the musty atmosphere of old chairs, he addressed the meeting.

He left after the first agenda, aware that all was not well with the more aggressive wing, but he thought he had balanced the occasion, and the New Front had not had it all their own way.

For the next hour Gerald steered a politician's course through the vicar's sweet reason to the free-for-all at the end. He would be interested to see whether special powers invested in members of the council could sweep clean an area of ground, moral or territorial, and bring to order so-called wicked men. For him it was an exercise, and he was the man, he never questioned, to head off any emotional stampede or fascist plot. He'd had enough practice with Jemima.

His two mates, brought for amusement and support at the time his wife disappeared were staying on for the promised festivities. These days they entertained Jemima and drank his whisky, proving a high price for help. But they lent power to his projects and the females showed interest and were on hand at all times, but he was not altogether in control. The experience was new to him. Later that night he contented himself by allowing Sylvia to flatter him with the merest hint of happy times to follow.

'Jemima's behaviour is a problem,' Sylvia announced. 'I don't know how you can live with it.'

'Perhaps I find it easier to live with it than live with her. Have you thought of that?'

He would not let her patronise. She thought of that and was disconcerted. It was her move and she was unprepared.

'Well, you must know what you can, what you both can...' there was another pause, 'tolerate.'

'Yes, that's why we have open house, open lives, I suppose, in her case,' he was careful to add.

'I'm going to get some more wine.' Sylvia needed time to reflect, she was leaving the room.

'Not for me. I must go.'

'You're walking. Go on, keep me company. Edward's seeing the Jeromes' home. They're perfectly capable of taking themselves back. Edward's the one who will have to return alone. He hasn't thought of that.'

'Are you seriously worried?'

'What about?'

'Burglars, hobos, people of the night. I recognise there is a real need in all societies to be extra vigilant about security and protection for the young, girls and women in particular. But I have never had the feeling of menace or threat round here. I am speaking as a man of course.'

'You know nothing, obviously. If you were to hear the daily gossip you might think on it further, I'm glad we can talk privately. We do so in public but obviously you are a little detached. I don't mean any criticism. We are grateful for the fact that you actually live here – most of the time anyway. But I could write a book.'

'Perhaps you should.'

'No, I must get back to this business of security.'

'I'm listening. Go on.'

'There is a handful of people in the town – no, not the town – from the hamlet, what they used to call the old village. One man in particular I have had trouble with. He used to be an employee until I discovered what he was.'

'I have heard rumours.' Bored with hearsay Gerald was prepared to get facts and finish the matter.

'In a word he destroyed my business and that includes the fabric of the building.'

'Really? What did he do?' What had started, as unrest was about to become melodrama?

'He destroyed, disfigured – well he painted – oh dear, the

83

walls!'

'Good God!' He saw he must not laugh. 'What colour?'

'No colour, but imagine the shock! He moved the furniture, changed the pictures, changed the business – would you believe, they were drinking in the streets. Then he raped my assistant.'

'Sylvia these are serious allegations. Have you proof? This must be substantiated.'

'I can show you the building.'

'I should be interested.'

'The assistant, she's young, heaven knows where she is now but her parents were most concerned. And she did have to have medical treatment. The local doctor can testify. He hasn't been approached yet.'

'You say "yet", is there a case?'

'If I have anything to do with it, yes. And that is not all. There is a drug problem; others involved, of course. There are fields of the stuff in the mountains. Only visible by helicopter. Now there are signs they are starting again. That man – the man I told you about is involved. He lives rough, I believe. We live in a jungle.'

'Good heavens.'

'Seriously, the worst thing is he is selling, or could be selling, drugs to the young.'

'Oh well, this puts a different complexion on the matter. I shall get in touch with the relevant authorities tomorrow. I can't think why I had not been informed of this before.'

'My dear Gerald, he is a local man. They close ranks. He is a popular figure. Popular, can you believe?'

'Where can I find him?'

'The Black Ox. Bottom of the town.'

'Does he drink there?'

'He works there.'

'He has a job?'

'He is never without a job. One person sacks him and another employs him again. It is a cabal.'

'I'm amazed at what you're telling me. Neither the police, the vicar nor the local authorities has said more than the casual reference you get on the street corner.'

'Ask my daughter. Just a minute, the girls are around somewhere.'

'Don't worry her now. Your daughter, you are telling me, knows him?'

'Knows him? They're mad about him, have crushes on him. You know what girls are.'

He paused, 'Yes, I'm sorry that your daughter is involved. Most distressing for you. What does your husband say?'

'You know Edward, he dismisses it. But I know what they're up to – Elida and Maddy, that is. Listen, they're here!'

'Not tonight, Sylvia. Tomorrow.'

He went home to the person best informed on the subject introduced that night. One he had chosen to ignore, one he hoped would not need his attention. He believed he had minimised damage to his career by distancing himself from his wife when possible. Now he decided her excessive and wilful behaviour made her an ideal receptacle for certain information too sensitive for the public ear.

Jemima was smoking and dyeing her hair.

'Don't come in.'

'I'm not going to.'

'Please don't. It'll go wrong.'

'Listen.' He closed the door he had partially opened and spoke to the woodwork. 'Listen. What do you know of drug dealing in Maesford?' He surprised her into attention.

'Ooh,' she stopped, turned off a tap, 'Not a lot.'

'Where?' he was shouting.

'Down the town. It's always down the town for anything like that. Go down the town.'

'Will you take me?'

'Whatever for?' He heard her laugh.

'Don't laugh. It's not a joke.'

'Yes. How funny.'

'Listen. I want to meet this man. Will you come with me?'

'What an offer. Scared to go alone?'

'Come on.'

'He runs The Black Ox. He's lovely.'

'Not according to Sylvia.'

'Oh, bloody Sylvia.'

'I say. Can I come in?'

'All right.' She opened the door, a towel and the collar of her bathrobe covered with dollops of black liquid. There were trails of the same substance on her face. As it dried it looked like blood. Her tangled hair fell in corkscrews to her shoulders.

'What colour is that going to be?'

'Red wine.'

'You look like a gorgon.'

'Oh. Get out.'

'I'm only joking. It will tone down.'

She put a towel over her head. Animal sounds, probably swearing were drowned by a gushing tap. 'Just get out.' She was angry.

'Come on. We can go for a drink.'

The promise of an encounter overcame his dislike of walking in the town accompanied by a character from Greek mythology. His wife could look quite pretty traditionally groomed but her frequent changes into what appeared to be fancy dress embarrassed him.

'Fine,' he said, and hoping that with time her present image would fade, he could put off The Black Ox to some point in the future, 'I'm seeing the vicar and the local doctor first.'

She left the tap splashing, hoping he would go away. He studied the remains of some wine in a dusty bottle, and wine glass on the dressing table, furred after days of private drinking. His wife had stopped to dab her eyes with yet another lotion. She sat on the bed, blindfolded in wet cotton wool. He tried to wash the dye-streaked basin, the toilet soap, and started on the glass.

'What are you doing? Leave it. I want a drink.'

She's a slut, he thought and put the glass down.

'Well, what did you want?'

'Come with me for a drink at the infamous pub.'

'On Wednesday.' He hazarded a day far off.

'He's a lovely chap. Everyone likes him.' Red-eyed, she stared in a mirror.

'Not everyone.'

'We could take the girls.'

'Christ, Jemima, haven't you listened to anything I've said?'

'What, damn you?'

'I've just spent an evening with Sylvia Bailey who insists he's corrupting her daughter.'

'Rubbish. It's rubbish.'

'That's not what she says.'

'It's a joke.'

'It's not a joke but I shall see for myself. Come on, you must try and understand my position.'

'Oh, your position.' Her contempt showed, he'd gone wrong with her again.

'Darling, please, a favour. I'll buy you dinner somewhere nice.'

'Not there.'

'I thought you said it was good.'

'Not "good", silly – bad, but he's a sweetie.'

'I hope I'm up to it.'

'I'm kidding. People like it. You'll like it. Yup!' She had wiped the stains from her face and her hair was beginning to dry. She looked bland as a child. 'Okay,' she added brightly.

He remembered when he had married her. He held her lightly and kissed her on a pale patch of skin.

'Oh, get off.' He hated her like this.

Gerald proceeded with care. The church was as helpful as he expected, taking both sides as the vicar deemed necessary. He appeared to lack drive when, in reality, he paused before coming down hard on an issue unweighed. In the world of checks and balances, he was seen to stand on the side of the loser and an effort to keep the peace. In this he was successful. It occurred to Gerald that he might be cleverer than once he supposed. Anyway he wanted him on his side, the more to discover what he knew than what he thought. Today the vicar was at his most unworldly. In his study, surrounded by flora, he appeared to favour botany. Gerald showed interest, then drew him towards politics. He guessed he had trespassed on a rare free hour and was brief. He said so, awkward in an awkward subject. The words in his head were rejected. They had been tossed around before at public meetings, no place for vice in the sunshine, in the sunshine of this airy room. The decent furnishings refuted deeds of Satan here or in the hills.

'I think not,' was the reply on all points.

'How can you be sure?' Gerald would say and was met with the same conviction.

'In my position I can be more sure than most. I listen and do not judge.'

'But you must have a duty to give information if there is crime. I imagine you think this way?'

'But I am aware of no criminal activities.'

'Are you just not aware?'

They were taking opposite sides and would not progress. He had now to apologise for impertinence, excusing questions he had been asked to pursue, and taking up a busy man's time.

'Mr Weatherstone, Gerald, we are both newcomers. I have been here a few years but not a few generations. The difference may be greater than you imagine. I try to be sensitive. Add to that the difference between town and country and you have another gulf. The place, delightful place, is another barrier. We may not be wanted here.'

'Surely that is a reason for staying, prevent civil war!'

'Oh dear, I hope not. Sometimes, I reject differences. If I sense a confrontation, I can proceed more easily by stealth. Your way is too overt for me. If I fail you can still go your own route.'

'Is there a reason why we should not work together?'

Gerald left. He liked things hanging in the air, knowing he could blow them away in a favoured direction. He was experiencing a power surge and went to interview the doctor.

The doctor lived in the centre of the town, in a house set back from the road. Joined to the shops by a low wall, topped with evergreens, an iron gate worn to rust, hung high on pillars, the gap below a free space where dogs and cats and paper could blow in. It was not considered a nuisance and afforded friendly access to the needy. People spoke of the doctor as if he alone were their support. Altogether, three made up the practice; an assistant and his assistant, a girl at the start of her career. The house was a gloomy place, dear to the doctor and his wife for all those characteristics other people hated.

'There's too much air outside!' the doctor was fond of saying when anyone closed a door, window or the large vent in the chimney. This unusual aperture could be shut by sliding a metal plate across the top whenever the fire was not alight. It rattled in the wind and proved his point, the doctor insisted, leaving the vent open and a downdraught in every season. In winter, heaters of various design stood around. Over the doors, on angled rails, curtains swung and shook in the air currents. If there was too much air outside, equally there was too much air within.

'A bit dark but restful,' said the doctor as Gerald groped his way. 'What was it you wanted to see me about? Not a matter of health I understand.'

'Not mine,' said Gerald.

The doctor paused on his way to three chairs. He seemed to count them, nodding his head before selecting one and indicating one for Gerald.

'It's about one of your patients,' he said, 'but before I go on I assure you I'm not asking for medical information.'

The doctor was a reticent man when not attending the sick and used silence like a sword. He was silent now. Gerald, who liked to lead, found entry into this conversation difficult. He felt on edge and doubted the justification for this interview. He had been forced into it as a final step before supporting Sylvia's case against the barman. A mother with a daughter, she had sent him off in all directions listing suspicions on four points. He thought it was four at the last count. Fear had grown like deteriorating weather, everything wrapped in a cloud.

'I won't take up your time. I'll be brief.' Could he be brief, he wondered? He had resolved to discuss the fate of various people. Now, more prudent, he would ask a question and get out. He sensed animosity before he started.

'Young people in the country have special problems, I imagine.'

'Oh no.' The doctor was not on his side.

'I have a friend with a young daughter.' He had taken the plunge.

The doctor, old in middle age, breathed contempt. Gerald wished himself away. The high gate with easy access was waiting for him. 'Has a concern,' he managed to go on, 'after a girl was attacked. As a local counsellor that's why I came.'

'Oh no.' The doctor remained unmoved, even disinterested.

'Really? You would have known, I suppose? The information wrong, exaggerated?' He had hoped for less monosyllabic speech.

As he made to leave, he tried a commonplace remark on the weather, followed by the view, in an attempt to draw another word from one claimed as the town guru.

'Yes,' the doctor said.

Irritated by now, Gerald would not give up. He risked all and jumped from gossip to scandal. 'In the conversation I recall, a school friend was assaulted, injured in some way, by a boyfriend perhaps, it's usually someone they know. Let's blame the television, another world out there. And not only out there. It's here it seems.' Gerald held out his hand, turned to leave during the silence.

'Oh?' The slow response brought him to the point again. He stated his case. 'Perhaps you would not necessarily hear.'

'I should hear.'

'I'm sorry. I am keeping you.' The door closed quietly behind him. For the first time Gerald felt he had made an enemy. He supposed he had handled it badly.

'I asked Sylvia,' Jemima said as they were walking down the road. 'She wouldn't come.'

'Did you really?' Her husband paused long between each word but sarcasm was lost on her. 'Did you really think she would come, to meet him socially?' He stood rooted to the pavement. His wife jerked to a halt.

'Why not?'

'You're a fool.' He walked on ahead of her. 'I should imagine she would prefer to forget him except that she is bent on revenge.'

'I didn't know.' Jemima shuffled behind him, a sulky child.

'You know now. And we're going for a quiet drink. You and I.'

'Okay, okay.' The thought of alcohol always cheered her up.

'I'm interested in this cult figure as he seems to have become. I must judge for myself before I put my name to any public action.'

'Forget it.' Anyway it was Sylvia's word.

Aledd stood behind the bar, his famous smile an invitation. In the time it took to contemplate a drink, Gerald had observed the man's appearance. Good-looking himself, he was loath to recognise good looks in another. But, he thought, as he considered it further, this was a face that generations had made.

'Come on,' Jemima was saying.

He ordered. Jemima leaned across a stool, weight on her elbows. The man turned away in the ritual of pouring a drink. Viewed from the side, he was stocky and country bred, but Gerald had seen enough to understand something, not to be called power, not guile, there was no artifice, he had simplicity. He was wrong, he was not a handsome man but he had an attraction. Talking to him later he decided it was simplicity that made him original.

'You're bored!' Jemima was fidgeting with her hair, twisting it into tighter corkscrews. Fearing a mad scene he decided to get her out. He was too late.

'Aledd.' She had caught the barman's eye. As he came forward, she held his wrist and slid her other hand to his elbow. She drew him down so that his face was near hers.

'Give us a kiss for Christmas. You are such a dish!'

'You are leaving.' Gerald was seconds away from trouble. In a second his wife would act the fool or tart, he never knew which side she would choose to show. At home he could deal with her, but not here.

'I'd like to take you back and put you under the tree. You're cute.'

Aledd blushed, but his composure was town smart, which could be dangerous Gerald thought, as he laughed a little, at the same time saying, 'You're not drunk. Don't pretend.' He called out, 'Goodbye,' as he would to a friend.

'I was going to buy you a decent meal, but not now,' he said to his wife as they left.

'Oh, go on. I was only joking. You know me.'

'I do know you.' Furious, he wanted a good time, and to talk, so he gave in. 'Are you going to behave like an adult?' She grinned and nodded.

'Well, do so... talking of adults,' he went on when she had quietened down, 'how old do you think he is – thirty, forty?'

'Don't know. He's older than he looks. Not more than thirty, not as much. I'll ask him next time.'

'There'll be no next time with me.' She was skipping down the road.

'For someone who is forty-seven you should know.' She stopped and turned a blank face to him. He recognised anger. They got in the car and drove beyond another restaurant, on towards home.

'I'm sorry,' she said. 'I didn't mean anything. Can't we have a meal?'

As he continued to drive he could see tears down the side of her cheek. He drove on for a while and pulled up a mile from the house and got out.

'What are you going to do?'

'Get you out.' He opened her door and pulled her gently by the arm.

'We're going to dinner but we're walking back, nearly back.' Her eye make-up had gone crazy. 'Look at your face!' He gave her a handkerchief.

'That's too clean,' she said.

Over food he got her sane and talkative. 'So that's your drug dealer.'

'You're joking.'

'No?'

'But he knows something.'

'Of course. It's a game for the kids in the village.'

'At the risk of sounding like a record – it's a dangerous game.'

'It's fun.'

'Tricky, and they will get into trouble.'

'There'll be no bother here!'

'One day there will.' He hoped she would take the hint but guessed she was too tight to care. He had one more go at her. 'I hope you don't still do it. I have a sense of self-preservation. You do not. I asked you today, because you know this scene, who runs things.'

'Nobody's running,' but she was running towards a mood that would swing out of control. Drinking, it was only drinking, had damaged her nerves. Her speech became shrill. 'Who's running?'

'I mean the little group.'

'Little group,' she mimicked.

He considered her for a moment. She should see a doctor, not in this town. One day they would both leave. They managed a meal in peace.

'Have you had enough?' She seemed to be falling asleep. He got the bill. In the fresh air she would revive. He walked her at a brisk pace through the wind to the protection of the car.

'Don't rush me,' she said in her child's voice. 'It's terrible.' In the car she fell in a heap. Unconscious, it took three of them to get her to her bed. His house guests looked embarrassed.

'Blame us, Gerald, we went to the golf club earlier and overdid it.'

'I know.' He felt relieved that their life was an escalator. At each floor, one or other of them got off, the last scene forgotten. Nevertheless he wanted to be remembered. This was his purpose as it was with most men he knew. He must make his mark. But it would not be here where the world had stopped half a century back.

Sylvia Bailey dulled his judgment. He needed to be where he could swim with the tide, ahead of the crowd, not where people disintegrated or devoured one another.

The phone rang. Sylvia's voice sang sweetly in his ear. His reaction surprised him. With speed he resumed his politician's role and believed her when she called him the chosen one to lead them to some sort of victory. He left his sleeping wife and went to a meeting. His two fiends spoke of departure. He would not be sorry. He needed freedom.

Aledd surrounded by a coterie of admirers, smoothed his shirt down across his thickening waist, adjusting his trousers. Some said he was getting vain. He stretched his arms and locked them behind his head. His face was fuller and coarser in the neck. He took a deep breath and resumed his former pose, hands on the bar. The times had transformed him. He had been given stature by his clientele. Their sophistication now was his. The fire that took him half an hour to light, glowed red and gold, reflecting his mood. He looked in the mirror. He noticed his hair was thinning. 'Responsibilities,' he told himself and decided to get a boy to help with the glasses. A woman already did cleaning. Lynne was not pleased. 'She's old enough to be my mother,' he told her. 'Well your mother and you are the same age!' Too amazed to be offended, he pursued the subject later at home. Lynne had left the room. He could hear a murmur of conversation.

'Listen, I'm not that much older than you.' He spoke loud enough for her to hear but she did not reply. 'Not that much,' he said again and went and stood in the doorway. She and his mother were at the sink.

'Tell her, Mam.' He studied their backs, side by side, both in a dark wool cloth like a uniform. The same height, the same except for the angle of the head, one held erect, the other bowed with a slope to the shoulders, his mother was often tired. They stood close together suggesting intimacy. He thought they might be laughing; women changed their mood like their clothes. But as Lynne turned he could see this was not so. She put down the towel and pushed past him.

'Hey,' he said backing away. 'Mam, tell her.' But his mother did not speak.

'Lynne, why are you angry?'

'I'm going,' she said. She struggled with the sleeve of her coat.

'Don't go like this.' He was used to acquiescence. Her determination made him uneasy. 'Don't go like this,' he repeated following her, his mother yards away, forgotten.

'Don't.' Lynne was threatening. 'You've done enough.' At once he was drawn back into their world of destruction.

'Why? Why now?' he was saying.

'You know why, you don't need to ask why.'

'We have been through this before.'

'Not this. Not other women. You're worse than Clifford.' He ran after her past two cottages down the lane until she disappeared into her own garden. It was too dark to follow her. At home he told his mother, 'I don't understand women, you know.' She

looked sadly at him. 'You're a good boy,' was all she said.
'What about Clifford?'
'Didn't she tell you?'
'Perhaps she couldn't.
Couldn't?'
'No, she couldn't.'
'Couldn't what? What did he do?'
'Ah well, you men don't know half of what you do.'
He hurt her? What did he do?'
'I won't say more.'

Her son stood at the table, a coat in his hand. He stood there a long time. When he sat and a mug was put in front of him he didn't drink, but something held him in the chair, an emotion that would not let him go. Now he understood her distance. It was the answer he half expected. He thought of nothing. He felt neither hunger nor cold. He got up finally and made his way in the direction of the town to a group of council houses near The Bell where he once worked. Cars passed him and a Landrover, new, unlike the farm vehicles. This town was on his doorstep but it was a land of strangers. He entered the bar, bright and warm. This was a popular pub, young farmers playing quoits and pensioners playing dominoes. It was difficult to get a drink. Standing at the back of a group waving money, he was able to look for the face of his enemy. The sea of faces, some familiar, became unfocused. He decided to get out. Then behind him through the door pushing him forward as it opened, two policemen came in, gleaming in their white shirts and polished buttons. Badges shone on their helmets making more light. Torches in hand, one beckoned the landlord who took them to a side room. The bar hushed. The silence broken by whispers made people uneasy. Innocent or guilty the intrusion struck fear into the company. Aledd tried to hear what they were saying. He slipped out.

From the iron pots in the farm shed, by the light of a lamp, he removed his secret from the old tobacco tin, and burnt it in the kitchen fire.

'What's that funny smell?' his mother wanted to know.
'Nothing, Mam.'

'I always know nothing means something with you!'

'No it doesn't!' He moved away to end the exchange. But his mother was following.

'Feeling better?' Her attention was out of character. Startled he looked to see her eyes shining in the glow of the bare bulb that hung on a rotting flex in the centre of the room, where it did no good. He thought he saw tears, tears for him, unexpected, never since childhood. Standing there opposite each other he experienced a sort of bond. He was not alone. He had a family, home and the land that extended upwards limitless. He had everything. This existed for a moment and in a moment it was gone. When he spoke his voice was rough.

'You must get those wires fixed, look at it!'

His mother made a sound like laughter, clearing her throat, returning to the other room, drying a glass, turning it slowly in her hands. She continued drying plates. He was aware of things he had not noticed before, the inverted cups and plates; dark, chipped on the draining board, odd spoons and forks. It was a poor collection but each was carefully stacked and charged with energy as if from within. Tomorrow it would be the same. It gave him comfort. His father was about somewhere. He could hear the hum of the television. He took some things from his mother's hands.

'What's got into you today?'

He knew he didn't have to answer. He sat sideways leaning on the back of a chair, enjoying the peace of·it. When the house was quiet and he was alone he went to the fridge and ate some cheese.

'Sexy Blonde Lady, Sophisticated, S.O.H.' Gerald's friend was reading aloud.

Gerald stuck without a secretary was only interested in personal columns as a means of checking business skills. 'What curious communications!'

They spoke in jargon, everyday a new vocabulary. He couldn't be bothered with it any more and wished they would leave.

'SOH, GWA.' They droned on. 'Do you know anyone without a sense of humour or who doesn't like animals?'

A face appeared at the window. Sylvia Bailey, hair blown in a mane, was tapping vigorously, her rings rattling the panes.

'Is it inconvenient? Hello, Stephen! Hello, Paul!'

'Sit down.'

She was obviously flustered. 'It's Elida, she's disappeared again!'

'What?'

'When I say disappeared, I mean she missed lunch and now it's teatime.'

'I'm sure you need not worry. She's probably shopping.'

'ATTRACTIVE MAN SEEKS ADVENTURE IN THE COUNTRY.'

'Oh please, not that. It's all been too much for me recently. I dread adventure. That's what we called it when we came here. I feel I'm sinking into a black hole!'

'DIVING,' Stephen continued and then in his turn, apologised. 'Forgive me. I'm lost in admiration of your adventures. I'm just seeking amusement to take me out of myself.'

'Rut,' said Paul.

'We're all in something. Look at Gerald.'

'A quandary!'

'Please.' Gerald was getting tetchy.

'Sylvia, do you ever read these advertisements. They give you a lift. DASHING YOUNG TYCOON IN THE MAKING.'

'Stop it, both of you.'

'POLITICS, ORIENTEERING, G.W.C.... C?'

'It makes one's hair stand on end.'

'I don't have hair any more, only a parting. Come on Gerald. What's your view.'

'Good God. I haven't one.' He saw with surprise they were tired of the bachelor run. 'Sometimes I envy you your single status.'

'Don't. We're together so much people think we're an item.' The elder brother warmed to his story. 'Once at the height of our matrimonial troubles, we left a bar, arm in arm. Paul was drunk, of course, he was crying, I think.' Paul growled. 'When two men came up and asked us if we'd like to swap, and a passing couple, mixed this time, said very loud, "How disgusting."'

'Be warned.' Gerald had the last word, 'You'll fly to New York with the one you choose, she'll drink too much and forget to return the ring you are sure to buy her.'

Sylvia had finished her drink. 'I shall go. I can see it was silly of me to come here. Sometimes just leaving the house is a cure.'

'Nonsense. Stay.'

'No. I'll leave you to your entertaining friends.'

'Take them with you if you like.' Joke though it was, the idea that someone else could take over was at last salvation.

'We're out.'

'Out?'

'Out!'

The afternoon wore on and when they left he was too alone. Jemima was out. Momentum gone, his work stalled. He saw each point of his agenda framed by the doubts he had let drift in with the low clouds that hung over the town. Golf was unpleasant in this weather, the air short of oxygen. It was part of the trouble. The atmosphere was not conducive to optimism. It darkened thoughts, made Swedes suicidal and Sylvia Bailey obsessive. It fuelled her belief that their town on the border was threatened. They were all on the border, beautiful but doomed. While his eyes scanned the computer image on his desk he planned what he would do. He would stop work, his conscience salved by the scheme he would conceive as he was heading down the town.

He hastened by the Bailey house, it still being an awkward hour for drinks that were always too available. Past the town shops, he slowed up by the famous inn – infamous now with so much gossip – its sign rusting the animal face to a sneer, and went on again to the old shop. Once part of a group quaintly clustered, it retained its name, 'the' and 'old' stressed according to meaning. Sheep cropped grass up to the door. He watched as they charged through the hedge of a rejected meadow. He had driven behind them for half a mile, a slow progress made slower by the farmer's strange load. With a rolling gait, he dragged a misshapen body spreading dust. Unexpectedly the animal sprang to life as it was chucked in the field. A dog barked, a boy waved.

He drew closer to the building. Stripped down to a plain structure, it looked embarrassed as if ill-dressed for a party. He peered in to see damp maps of fungus circling the walls. A little shocked at the speed of its decline, he studied the outside. The FOR SALE board had slipped. At the back, mortar was crumbling.

Some storage sheds and stunted trees led directly onto the marshland with a view to some hills. He wandered through weeds to a wall, wind lashed. The dismal fogs of Sylvia's description looked ornamental, blowing like smoke along the tracks of the higher ground. By now he had recovered some of his good weekend mood. A log fire and something to eat would round off the day, a time to reassure himself that he was successful. He went to the top of a small rise and stood, like the cattle in a field below, blowing funnels of warm air that curled in the frost. The temperature had dropped. Leaving the car, he strode, bent double, hands in pockets back to the town and The Black Ox.

There was the fire and the usual crowd, he supposed, being a stranger. They all wore caps. One he had seen before wore his at a sharper angle, nursing an eye, injured, he imagined by some vicious piece of farm machinery. Their clothes were black as coal. Coal was in their skin from the fire of the cottages. Coal on their breath. They stared into their beer. The man opposite smoked open mouthed, the cigarette stub like a wart on his lower lip. Gerald moved to the bar. No one except the barman spoke. Mindful of their last meeting which seemed forgotten, he was glad of a friendly face, and Aledd's voice that rolled on with hardly a pause did not invite responses. It had rhythm and depth which, more than words, made the minutes pass and strange become homely under the shaded lights.

He intended only to have one drink but the pint slipped down easily. The beer was thick and sweet. He sat down to the next one and discussed things of no consequence.

In time the group by the fire got back to the subject of the day in a language of their own. As pints were pulled, some money was exchanged but mostly a record was made in a book behind a bottle. The fire was giving out scorching heat. Occasionally a remark, sharp in repartee, was followed by a laugh. Chips were thrown to a dog.

Gerald knew he aroused suspicion. He looked different. They, on the other hand, now he had studied their faces, all looked alike. Sylvia called all her numerous gardeners 'Glyn' and, when questioned, offered this simple explanation. He guessed she was possibly right, they would all nod in assent. It was true. They were all related. In remote areas people were united. He saw the same squared features, the same serious or artful expression, sons, fathers, brothers, drawn together, closed. He began to experience a reaction to this subculture that had charmed him at first. It was his job, he told himself, part of his job, but he had difficulty in adjusting. He felt the eyes of the barman on him, sensing his discomfort which had drawn him out of his role. He was persuaded when he first came through the door that he could be part of a world where the smell of hops and wood smoke cocooned him. Awakened as from a reverie, now he was aware he was an intruder and even a foe.

'How do you like this after London?' Aledd was reassuring him in a role reversal.

'It's beautiful but town people find it hard to settle in the country.'

'I wonder why?'

'I don't know.' After a while he went on, 'A new life is absorbing, then the novelty wears off. They feel lost and cling together for comfort.'

'Oh do they? I didn't know that. We just live, you see. The place is part of us. I can't see it any other way. We're all part of it, aren't we?'

'Are we?'

'Are you ordering something to eat?'

'No, I have a meeting.'

Gerald left without furthering his investigation and without food. He had forgotten hunger in the smoke-filled room and without a notion how he could again approach a man so cool and unaffected. However he had built a bridge.

As the year wound down, shops still with their 'back soon' signs, brimmed with holly and mistletoe, trees and wreaths. The festooned doorways and choked pavements forced pedestrians in circular tracks onto the road, uncomfortably near the traffic. Drivers sighed and slowed remembering goodwill. CAR TRANSPORTER DRIVER PLEASE DO NOT HIT THIS HOUSE was noted more carefully.

'I've never seen so much mistletoe,' Sylvia said, 'it tells you something.'

She was in a relaxed mood despite the seasonal blight when her daughter could be relied upon to hide herself away. Shut in her room, barred against all comers for the greater part of each day, she indulged in a 'prolonged adolescence', her mother's phrase.

'No amount of mistletoe will bring her out!'

Edward felt for her. Walked in the garden. When indoors, complained of berries in the food and general discomfort. Decorations were an embarrassment, even salt and pepper were disguised as nests instead of recognisable containers.

'Pearls...' said Sylvia, as something dropped in the wine, and mouthed the rest of the sentence.

'She may or may not be witty,' said her husband, 'but she will have the last word. And she's not alone,' he went on, addressing the chairs, 'it must be the reason some people can never leave a room. All over the world there are people standing in groups waiting for a suitable exit line.'

'Shut up dear, don't be theatrical, leave that to me!'

'And by the cars. In the rain...'

'He's light-headed, something's changed him,' her mind ran on, but her Christmas spirit, as happy as a child's, brought her back to the world of sugar and candles. 'I must say you are talking again. I like it!' Her voice rose claiming the last word as she went.

The telephone in the hall was ringing.

'Yes, Ben. We haven't forgotten our carols.' Her words floated clear as bells.

Edward put down his paper. There was a silence suggesting change.

'"Yes" to the church, "no" to the other place,' she went on. 'Definitely "no" to the other place.' Conversation continued at the other end. 'I'll think about the third idea.' She had wandered back, the phone on her shoulder, twisting the watch on her arm, arranging her sleeve. 'I'm dashing.' The phone was placed on the sofa where she sat.

'How could he!' She was angry now. 'Would we go there!

Would anyone think to sing hymns in a pub?' After a little pause, 'With that man.'

Edward did not ask which man but concluded, 'It's all in the past.'

'It's not!'

'Oh dear!' He was reading the paper again. 'But we're all singing carols, I hear!'

'Yes and you're coming, I mean, are you?'

'So long as it's not outside.'

'No, we haven't arranged outside yet.'

'Well, I'm not one for outside singing, remember.'

'Remember, remember, the 5 November. How funny they don't have fireworks here.'

'Probably because it would frighten the sheep.'

'Thank goodness it's Christmas. I hate long periods of in-activity.'

'Farming is full time.'

'There seem to be troughs of low pressure, troughs and flat periods drifting on. It used not to be like this at home, I mean in the old days, drifting.'

'You do more here.'

'The daily round, domestic things.'

'Domestic, do you mean jam?'

'Next year, and I have only just decided it this minute. Perhaps it was you saying, "jam" – jam is WI, my dear.'

'Oh.' This was the way he liked it, the family at home – rare – and conversation unchecked by politics. 'Oh,' he said again, comfortably screened by the paper.

'It's just come to me. In the New Year I shall open the shop again.'

She ran up the stairs. A draught crept round Edward's newspaper.

The heat in The Black Ox was fierce. As Rev. Ben Tooley had experienced this before, at the Harvest Supper, he knew what to expect. But the room was a cauldron even with the fire banked under sawdust. Inhabitants found it unremarkable. Enthusiasm raised temperatures. People jockeying for position at the bar sent ripples round the room. 'Vicar!' a voice cried. 'Wait a minute.' And more beer was pulled. It beat The Bell up the road. The crowd swayed. The vicar grateful for the turnout quietly gave thanks and fearing his strength would fail, prayed again within himself for stamina. 'Vicar,' they cried again and a bottle of misty liquid, passed from face to face, arrived in his hands and he swallowed, prayed and passed it on down the line.

Here were the old words and the old tunes played by Aledd at a fine pace, and Nancy 1 and Nancy 2 when he went to serve drinks. The vicar expecting two men, never forgot the shock, experienced again as at this moment the ladies, beautiful in a shifting mellow light, played them back into a time past. For a moment he felt outside it. The heat had made him unwell. He pulled himself through by an effort of will and movement of his arm towards a gap opening and closing. Pressed forward he had the feeling he was leaning on a cloud. It was useless to call for quiet. Minutes passed.

'The lesson will be read by someone long past their bedtime.' Quite young children were present, grasped round the waist by their fathers or sitting on their mother's knee. Hands clapped, glasses clattered, the community united. Those privileged to sing solos were rinsing their throats in advance and arranging lines of drinks on the bar for their reward and relaxation later. Old ladies and attentive daughters, guided to the fire, sat in easy chairs and played their part, stacking and raking. Ash flicked into the air from time to time, settled on the glasses and covered the tables and trouser legs of the swarming crowd.

Aledd caught the eye of Nancy 1 and, excusing himself, made the kitchen and by way of the back door, escaped into the street. The cold night was a blessing he believed. He gulped in fresh air and went to the front entrance. He opened the door a crack to encourage the incomers, should it be possible for them to get in after others had made their way out. Now he could stand at the back.

'Is that snow or what?' someone shouted.

He was forced outside again. Lynne might arrive but would not venture in alone. He looked up the road. She was not there but would come he was sure. A heavy rain rang with a sound like metal pellets on the street. He could hear the vicar announcing another hymn, knowing a good sing was worth more than a sermon in these conditions. Every face smiled. The unaffected pleasure was in contrast to the style of the top church on the hill. There were difficulties in singing hymns in foreign languages. Welsh was strong but the translation – 'All poor men and humble, all lame men who stumble' – came uneasily from the mouths of the Jeromes a week ago.

German, the vicar had allowed, but Dutch and French had proved too taxing. 'Learn the words and we'll try next year!' he had said and closed the book. 'Oh dear!' From where he was standing, it sounded and looked like Gerald Weatherstone's wife. Perhaps he had been hasty.

Back in the present, he noticed the Bad Ellises had gone. Bashem and Fishhook were the first to notice something happening in the cellar. Creeping down to find a free drink they had found water already inches deep. 'Help,' they cried, knowing diversion would cover their movements. 'Quick everybody.'

The crowd surged to the bar and looked over. Those at the back leaned on those at the front. Glasses broke on flagstones.

'Be careful now. You're making it worse, and please remain seated!' seemed a vain request as people pushed in three directions. Aledd dragged Lynne, who was cowering on the doorstep, to the centre of the room where the vicar and Gerald stood fast. The ladies tried to leave, pushing Aledd back to where he started. Girls made for the toilets through the coffee room or stood on chairs.

On the opposite side, in a private corner with settles, three men who had renewed their beer order, doubled to save time, held six pints like torches above their heads. Struggling to their table, foam lathered their hair.

'Open the door,' said someone. Aledd sent for the fire brigade.

'Make a human chain! Make a human chain!

We're chained already! We can't move!'

'Get in, Father. Get in Father.' The new Irish priest loved a hooley.

'If I get in any farther I'll be out the other side!'

Excitement sent the crowd into a manic dance. Some were

jumping for a better view. Music began again. 'O come all ye faithful.'

'We don't want any more people.'

'Thank you, Nancy,' said the vicar. 'Not now, later, when we've breath.'

'This is the best introduction to country life.' His hand was on Gerald's shoulder.

Jemima, it seemed, had not left her husband and was serving drinks. Aledd pushed Lynne behind the bar saying, 'Stay with Mrs Weatherstone.'

'Come on, love, you take the money and I'll pour.'

Aledd went outside and looked at drains. A voice said, 'The road's blocked. The river's rising. It's running over the common. The Bad Ellises' cottage had been flooded for days. Situated in a deep valley by a stream, cottages occupied by the extended Ellis family were notorious for flooded floors. As winter progressed the family with cats and dogs settled on higher levels, the bedrooms mostly. The Bad Ellises, it was known, lived by their wits. As the police arrived they were seen running with their cronies through the back door which relieved the pressure a bit. It was noticeably colder.

'Can we have sandwiches, now?'

'Silence for the vicar!'

'The vicar will say grace.' The soloists bawled above the chaos. The vicar, making a practical point, suggested they sat down or stood by a table.

'What about chips?'

'No chips?'

'No cooking while we're under water!'

'Sit down!' the soloist yelled again.

With the arrival of sandwiches, silence fell, followed by the murmur of people, talking with their mouths full. Rev. Ben Tooley gave a blessing while he had his congregation captive. Gerald Weatherstone praised the community spirit and the fire brigade arrived. Everyone clapped as they trouped through the parting crowd to the dark waterlogged cellar.

Aledd in the doorway once more dripped water and mud. He stood like a statue for some time. No one looked in his direction.

All eyes were on the pumps and sandwich plates. At length he crossed to the spluttering fire. There was a steady march of uniformed men and their admirers who followed like a flock of birds, flying and alighting at each point of the clean-up. Aledd was discovered by two women who patted him with mats and tea towels. He bore their giggles. He looked very cold.

'Can't someone find you clothes?'

Jemima predictably found some. A chill crept round the floor. The fire had at last succumbed to beer and water. In the time it took to recognise disaster, some moments or minutes of shocked commiseration, the earlier scene of so much rejoicing had turned to desolation and despair. Winter was upon them.

The crowd had gone. Ben, remembering his wife, fled, struggling up the hill with a borrowed umbrella. Only Aledd remained with his girlfriend and the Weatherstones, abandoned in the leaking room. The bad boys of the town could be heard foraging in the dark. Lynne thought she caught a glimpse of a woman, her hated rival, outside the window and clung more tightly to Aledd's arm.

'You mustn't let this overshadow the success of the evening.' Gerald chose this moment to make a speech. 'It must be a disappointment to you. Clearing up will take time. You have put a lot into this. We have heard of the changes you have made.' There was more in this vein, praise and appreciation. 'The pub used to be part of the old village, didn't it?'

'Yes, and the chapel. There was the church. The Ellises' two cottages. The rest disappeared.'

'You like him?' Jemima remarked on the way back.

'I suppose I do. Sylvia won't approve. I shall be called a turn-coat and she will report me to the committee if I'm not careful.'

'Whatever for?'

'For putting the village before the town, perhaps. I'm here to further business interests and may have favoured too much the feelings of the other side.'

'Not like you!'

'I know it's not like me! I'm being affected by something like ghosts from the old place. A joke! We'll soon be in London. Don't fret.'

'I may not want to go to London. I like it here.'

'You do now but next week this will just be an experience, the vicar's gig. You won't like the silent winters. People meet up for something like this. Go home and we won't see them again. They melt into the mist. Look, as we walk up the hill something is changing.'

'No, silly!'

'When we get out of the car. Drive for five minutes, it'll change. You'll feel differently. I'll ask you.'

'I don't think so!'

'I do. Do it and in a few minutes I'll ask you. Don't think about it. You drive. Go on, you drive. This is my experiment.' He threw her the key.

'You're daft but I'll do it. Okay.' She climbed into the driver's seat. Nearing their destination she said, 'Well?'

Home, they flopped onto a leather sofa designed to relax and inhibit movement. The central heating was high.

'What do you want?' he said, 'Whisky? Coffee?'

'Nothing.' She sounded low.

'Now tell me, what price the country pub?'

'I dunno, I'm tired.'

'But do you want to live there. Work there. Work on a farm?'

'Why ask me when I live here?'

'Here is not there. Here could be anywhere. We're surrounded by modern comfort. There, just a few miles away is fairyland. I'm asking you, could you live like the people there, understand them, be happy even?'

'Why on earth ask me that?'

'Because I want to know if you know, because I don't.'

'Gerald, don't ask me.'

'All right, birdbrain.'

'Don't pick on me. What have I said?'

'Nothing, that's the trouble.'

'Every evening ends like this. Maybe I could live there but certainly not with you. Goodbye, Gerald. Have a nice Christmas.'

'I'm sorry. Forgive me.'

'Gerald, it's too late.' She swayed out of the room. She was asleep when he went up. He guessed she would leave in the morning. He could never talk to her. He thought of Sylvia Bailey, the nearly literate, the hardworking, socially obsessive, keen, and confidant. There she lay in her designer bed in the house on the top of the hill. He could see the light that she'd extinguish before midnight. Up at seven, she'd fight through another fruitless day. He could phone at eight thirty. An earlier call might signal an emergency. Jemima was an emergency on legs, so predictable it bored him. This time it was his fault but he no longer cared. Damn her. Damn all women. Sylvia Bailey was a cow. He was depressed. He knew what it was. He sensed that something had ended. He felt it before when his parents died, but this time he recognised it, as it was happening, sharp and final. He was miserable. The place had bewitched them. He knew quite well it was rubbish, of course, but it was the way people spoke. The place was making them all unstable because they believed it.

Coloured bulbs on a wire, repeated down the street, on the centre of each strand a hook to hang an object, cheerful, symbolic, made an appearance each December as Maesford prepared to celebrate Christmas. It might seem a muted event to the outside observer, but in a land where animals outnumbered people it was festive enough. On the inside, the longed-for day would come when work-tired people broke their routine to erupt in a joyful exuberant fiesta. Religious or pagan or plain and simple fun, the time and place and particularly the way this was expressed, was worth the twelve-month wait. That was the general opinion.

'If they don't hurry up it will be Easter,' was a repeated comment that exasperated the vicar who had stars, he told them in the garage. 'Angels and Shepherds are ambitious,' he reflected aloud. 'Lambs!' said a child. 'There you are,' continued the critic, 'there's Easter for you.' People reacted variously. Gerald gave his wife's present to Sylvia. 'You shouldn't but Jemima is preposterous and has only herself to blame.' Lynne bought Aledd a red polo neck sweater. The vicar, his popularity high, received a whole pig from his parishioners, themselves overwhelmed by food and drink. The sparkle of Christmas trees in windows glowed for a time and as suddenly went black again when night enclosed them until dawn rolled down like a grey carpet.

Since the flood, Aledd's depression, a twinge at first that grew like an ache inside him, soon was to control each day and leave him sleepless. His job gone again, the pub dank and hollow, he took care to avoid that part of the town and threw himself into work on the farm at home, as if driven by demons. He was used to one routine, could not easily create for himself another and with a sense of loss brooded in silence.

'When will it end?' he said to Lynne one night.

For her part, she began to fear these conversations when he was in a low state and spoke in ways she couldn't understand, sometimes talking to himself.

'I wish you'd tell me what's the matter,' she would say, and he always answered, 'how can I tell you when I don't know.'

One day he announced he was taking a holiday. The effect was immediate, like a blind raised. His optimism, his smile, his light step were present again and he sought the company of acquaintances, relaxed with them as if he had never been away. He would work on the farm, his old life made new, doing odd jobs when odd jobs were there to be done. First he bought clothes and walked round the old village and up through the town on the opposite hill.

Sylvia Bailey heard from her daughter that The Black Ox was closed and gave thanks. Elida felt her contact with the real world was lost and despaired again. Her mother in contrast skipped down the hill to revamp her shop. She took down the FOR SALE board and planted shrubs.

'Wonderful,' she told her husband, 'to go past the place' – she gave the words heavy emphasis so there would be no mistaking the particular location – 'without feeling malign forces coming out at you from behind the windows. I always felt I had to accelerate there' – again the emphasis – 'just to escape.'

Edward rustled the papers on his desk.

'Have you ever felt there was something really bad about a place? Not just this place, any place?'

'No, Sylvia,' he said and thought he had ended the conversation.

'I may be silly,' she was going on.

'My dear, if it affected you so strongly, I'm surprised you haven't moved.'

'I nearly did six months ago.'

'You didn't mention it.'

'Didn't I? I suppose I didn't want to upset you, you liked it here but as you have often said, you like it anywhere.'

'Not quite anywhere.'

'Well, with your things and a view.'

'Yes, I suppose that is enough.'

'Anyway, everything has changed.'

'It must be spring.'

'Hardly!' She made one of her exits.

With new clothes and a girl at his side, a new man, Aledd walked down the town. The road had emptied of traffic. Maesford was a desert. The warden, in charge when the lights failed, had got it wrong again. With all lights at red for much of the time, there was no sense of locomotion. He went into shops, made modest purchases, entered the top pub where he had pulled his first pint. Lynne, at his side, drew back. He caught her hand. Feeling her draw back, he pulled her in with his old laugh and asked how they were doing. The place had been newly painted. The owner growled a reply from the back but Aledd was not to be thwarted.

'Don't be like that, I came to see how you were getting on.'

'No thanks to you!'

But he had turned to a small group of men Lynne had never seen before and disliked enough to move away. There was laughter and muted talk before they left.

'Why did you take me in there? It was horrible.'

'There was someone I wanted to see.' And he added, 'I wanted to show you off.' They crossed the road to a parade of shops.

'Who were those men?'

The hill was steep at this point and he covered his answer with puffs of breath.

'No one – business – nothing important.'

'They were nasty.'

'Don't be silly. I'll buy you coffee, tea, at a cake shop if you like.'

'No. I'm scared. You were different when you were with them. I want to go home.'

'Was I? Come back to the farm.'

'Is your mother in?'

'I dunno. Why do you want to see my mother?'

'I don't feel safe here any more.'

'How old fashioned.'

'I'm not. You were the one who was old fashioned. That's why I liked you!'

'Me, old fashioned?'

'In some ways. Certain ways!' she laughed.

Her laughter disconcerted him and he was silent, embarrassed.

'Tell me.' But she had disarmed him. Now he had lost his earlier swagger. 'Never mind.' Pleased, she pressed him further to calm a fear that threatened to spoil their day.

'What's happening? Just now in the pub you were a different person.'

'We all change.'

'Don't change.' But they had both experienced one.

The world changed with lighter days. People came out of their houses. Gardens grew green. Shops had customers. And like the animals roaming further afield, Aledd took to the hills. His van was seen everywhere. 'There he goes,' they said, 'he must be making a fortune.' He worked at home and at unspecified jobs on other farms from time to time, to pay for his keep.

'You mustn't stay here,' his mother said, 'you can't live on air!'

'I've saved,' he said, 'and I don't eat much. That's all right, isn't it?'

His father's health had declined in the hard weather. For months rain had penetrated the old building, made the hills impassable and lanes and tracks wretched quagmires of black slime. 'You need me here.' Aledd exchanged a look with his mother that was an answer.

He would return to the wilderness. The pleasure it afforded him was compensation enough for the loss of prestige he once had gained, not just in his own eyes but also in those of others. There were certain people of standing in the town he liked to call his friends. The female view in favour of barmen would turn to contempt at the thought of a tramp. Was he a tramp spending days, sometimes nights in the hills? He took care to wear his best clothes in the town, particularly if he went to make contact with the men whose business both scared and fascinated him. Here he saw money and an unknown world his mother worried about. One word, he was told, could secure a cash reward but at some risk. A strong sense of danger saved him so far, and a shiver of fear when bored and he contemplated adventure, sent him racing to his crumbling cabin where he toiled, building and digging to make something of his life. He was, he assured himself, making something. Now his visits to the town were few.

Elida Bailey's visits to the town were also coming to an end. At The Black Ox, shuttered, she stood shocked at the doorway. No familiar face at the window welcomed her in. She waited for a moment and looked at the contents of her smart tote bag to cover her nerves before returning home. 'Where's he gone?' she asked, near to tears. Her mother was deliberately unhelpful.

'Don't ask me. Why on earth do you want to know?'
'He was the only person who was ever nice to me.'
'Good heavens!' said Sylvia, ending all discussion. She came back minutes later. Maybe she was too hard on her daughter. 'Darling,' she started. Elida looked suspicious. 'Come and help me with the shop. You know I'm starting again. Antiques, no cakes and bread – silly regulations – maybe materials, what do you think?' Her daughter did not react. 'Come with me. Not today of course.'

It was spring and the sheep were back. Nothing ever had felt this right. 'Spring,' Aledd whispered. The sheep were noisily cropping turf. He had made a decision to change his life and it was well. He boiled a kettle and ate cheese and an onion pie found in the fridge. It didn't matter to his mother what he consumed, either at home or what he took to the mountain. She gave him everything but he would make it up to her he told himself. Today was too good for doubts. He mused on past happiness, but could not quite remember so much peace. The nights were still cold and as the light faded he prepared to leave, sad the day must end. He kicked at the fire and watched it die and stamped it flat before leaving. Checking his things and pockets for the van key he heard a movement outside. He paused bent over his pile of possessions and listened, aware of something alien, a sound more insistent than the soft drift of cattle or sheep. He froze, bent over the ashes. Nothing stirred the coarse grass in the stones, nothing shifted or snapped. He kicked the fire again and fanned the sparks. He stamped heavily on the fire making the dust fly as a voice said, 'Don't do that.' He froze a second time bent lower and knew he must straighten his back and accept whatever came next. He didn't turn.

'I thought we'd find you here.'

Seconds passed. When he looked there were two of them. He stood braced, his feet apart waiting for the inevitable. Out of silence and deep shadows came shock waves. His heart pounded.

'You don't look pleased to see us.'

Only one spoke. The other walked away kicking at the loose stones on the floor. Aledd knew them, of course he knew them. The roughness of the voice had confused him.

He was thinking more clearly. There was no danger at present. Yet there must be danger. He could feel its sharp thrust, and he knew then there was no escape for him now his hiding place was discovered. Trapped with them he would be drawn in, caught, punished, for greed and a game of dare.

'Well we've found you now.' The taller one did the talking.

'This little place you have taken so much trouble with is perfect, isn't it?' The thin face relaxed in this moment of triumph. Aledd breathed more freely again, prepared to hope that life might return to normal. The other man 'yeah-yeahed' in agreement.

'You didn't tell us, did you?' The mood changed back.

'What do you want?' It was all Aledd could say, struggling to take control. It would be more difficult to shift them than drunks in a pub. 'You're here now,' he continued and waited.

'Yeah,' he heard from the man in the corner.

'We're here and we'll stay.'

'You can stay if you like. I'm off. It's too cold. You'll find it's too cold at night.'

'Stay, Aledd.' Aledd knew it was an order. The men drew close and looked as though they might force him to the wall. Aledd was stronger but not stronger than two. He sat on the end of a table, wondering if he looked casual.

'Right.'

'You're more sensible than we thought. Isn't he, Sean?' The man's name he remembered. He shifted his position. 'Don't show yourself outside.'

'There's no one there but sheep. Don't worry.'

'I do worry. You're wrong. There's always somebody out there. You should know.'

'I give in. What do you want?'

'I'll get to the point. You and your place. We'll pay.'

All this he knew. 'I don't want paying.' Is this what he had planned? He could not imagine, in his quiet misery, why he had done it. He might comply, but he must not be blackmailed. He was bargaining for his life. This way he could win, he was confident. But he was never more afraid.

'All this free. It isn't mine. If you want it take it.'

'We're taking you too.'

'You're crazy.' Aledd looked into drug-dilated eyes. The man looked wild. 'You're crazy to think I can help you. I'm local but I don't know anything. I know nothing and I like it that way.'

'You know plenty. Know nothing? You know a lot.'

'I don't.' All he wanted was to escape. He had the van keys in his pocket now but daren't indicate he had transport. There was a chance the van was unnoticed, hidden in the rocks, part of his plan, for a secret life. On the TV, he would throw one man the keys and beat the other at a run, but it might not work in real life. At this moment he knew what real life was and decided to keep the keys.

'Want to hear the plan?'

An envelope that could contain money was thrown on the table. If he took it, he was lost, if he refused it, he was conceivably dead. Was that what he feared when apprehension first shook him, minutes ago? He was decided now. He took the packet.

He took it and it burned in his pocket. He had escaped, his body whole. He'd escaped with his life and earned a torture.

At home, he hid the money he didn't want in one of the iron pots at the farm and placed the pot back on the step by the door. Last year's withered flowers blown to shreds still trailed in webs over one side. He would spend time at home now and made pretence of gardening, although he longed to be walking mountain paths. He feared the sight of strangers. Apprehension was back to haunt him for ever. He recognised its fine signs like a prick or a flash of light. He would start out of his composure at the sound of footsteps and an enforced journey into town left him weak. Lynne admitted he was making her miserable again.

'Leave him alone,' was the general response.

'He's been no good for you.' And if she demurred. 'Just keep away.'

A prisoner in the confines of the farm, he felt helpless. It was more difficult to assess his situation. He would never understand the reasons for his predicament. One day, stronger and determined, he marched out to offer his services in some way back at the pub again. Free to face the people he feared, he at least had the protection of employment and an anchor. He worked and waited and began to feel secure until the day they came for him and forced him up into the hills. In the land of rocks and streams that were once his joy, his head swam and he choked on the words they dragged from him until his head swam. He was being recreated, a monster puppet that complied, near to breaking. He hoped in some part he was still true to himself as he said, 'Yes. Okay, I will,' and praying meant 'no'.

He was left to walk for hours, his legs weak. He made for the chair by the kitchen table where before he had found relief. But what he thought was pain before had been only vanity, gratification, greed. He put his head on his arms and surrendered to the emptiness inside him.

He tried to find Lynne. She was out. He left a letter for her on the stove where she might find it before her mother burned it. There was no one around. He went on to the town. To appear unconcerned, he read a newspaper on a rack and considered returning home to the empty house again. He felt cold and hot in turn and wondered if the sweat that pricked his body had broken out on his face. Once home he would have lost this resolve. He must go forward, wherever it took him.

The police station like a cottage looked empty. Suddenly, the world had become unpeopled. A door stood open. Pushing it back and stepping inside, a small area like an office held a table and chairs. Another door opened into a room with file-lined walls. Through the window, daylight washed away the threat and he was about to leave when a uniformed unfamiliar figure came and sat formally at a desk.

'Is Clive here?' he asked, and suiting the occasion, 'Clive Willis.'

'Later. He's at head office up the town. How can I help you?'

'No, it's a bit personal.'

'I see,' said the constable. 'As you're making it official, perhaps you can give me some facts or the nature of the business and I can pass them on.'

'No. It's to do with the hill farms. He knows the one I'm talking about, I best discuss it with him. I'll wait.'

'Take a seat.' He sat for a long time in silence until his em-embarrassment made him move to the outer room and from there into the street. He walked home counting the number of paces and walked back counting the number again, in case thinking would make him change his mind. He threw the packet of money on the desk.

'You've got to help me,' he said. 'You told me to come to you and I have. I must talk to Clive.'

'One moment.' A conversation, brief, staccato, whispered in the office, brought Clive and the constable, who left him with Clive, and the relief was immediate, help and safety. He sat weakly like a patient before his doctor.

'Who can you trust, Aledd?' Clive said finally, when Aledd slumped miserably back in the chair. And answering his own question continued, 'There's some you can trust more than others. You're not a family man – luckily.'

'Perhaps I may be. I feel I am. I feel I am. We've been here for generations. You too. We have a hold.'

'Let's hope it's strong.'

'Of course.'

'You hope.'

The knowledge of those years was strength on his side. In this aspect he had won.

'We rely on some,' was the policeman's last word.

He advised him to go back to work. That is, if he still had a job. Aledd worked part-time in comfort. Then after one day he decided protection doubled the threat, multiplied it. He insisted the police should talk to his mother and Lynne.

'Just a chat.' He tried to sound unconcerned. 'While I'm in the melting pot.'

He saw people hurrying in the street, convinced they avoided him. He never went to lonely places. There were people there, he imagined looking idly around like the cattle, but in reality looking for him. One warm day, frustrated by this exile, he sought out the shepherd and with a companion for an hour, wandered and sat like mountain sheep in a cave and on some slate flats lay in the sun.

'You were silly,' said his companion, breaking into his dream, 'you should have given the money back.'

'How?'

'Put it back in the old barn.'

He thought for a while. 'It's too late now.'

'No it's not,' said the shepherd. 'Ask Clive.'

'You're a genius.' Aledd jerked his feet.

Running down paths that sloped steeply to join the main track, he left his friend and rejoined the noisy world. He wondered how he could have been so stupid not to have thought of it before. Once he had given the money back, he could consider himself free. He felt liberated already. He meant to visit the shining water, his most private place, but events changed too fast.

Now he was back at the bar, working in a time loop, warm, placid.

'Pulled the body of a girl out of the "Mawn Pool",' someone was saying. No one knew who it was. Aledd's sight blurred as they spoke. Beer formed another pool over the side of the glass.

'Not known,' they said, and his vision cleared.

He left the protection of the bar and moved among the tables to a point behind a familiar figure. He recognised the downward slope of a farmer's cap.

'I tell you now I was shocked.'
'Yes!' It was easy to join in.
'You're looking better boy.'
He treated the man to a smile.
'No clothing anywhere. Not a sign of a struggle.'
'Murder!'
'Tourists.' Laughter now, then voices low.
'It's not that deep,' Aledd said and all eyes were on him.
'A bad place.'
'No place for strangers.'
'A good place,' Aledd interrupted.
'Not for strangers.'
'Not for strangers.'

He weakened and turned away, confused that he had created a tourist attraction. 'It was,' he once told an admiring crowd, 'rain water in the peat, a refreshment for travellers and cattle.' He had also given it magic and powers, he blushed to remember. But that was in the past. He dismissed the thought. He was not responsible. At home, he heard the news no one could have anticipated of Sylvia Bailey's daughter.

That night he smoked and counted the pills a nurse had given him. The doctor had told him he wasn't depressed but unhappy from too many misfortunes. If it was fate that he must suffer, perhaps it was fate that he must die. Fate had provided the pills. If he must die, must he take a hand in it? He saw Elida who lay in the glassy waters of the mountain, her long hair floating like a picture he once saw of a girl with flowers. He thought of flowers and took one of the pills. He slept but the misery would not go. His eyes were bad and something in his head was heavy. People asked if he were ill.

'You must rest,' they said. 'You don't look so good.'

Always talking, too much talk. No peace, no good sounds. Voices like machinery, beating hard, metal sheets sliding forward and back. Outside the wind was full of frightened animal cries. On the farm, lambs shrieked held in pens, pale and black, their faces packed together. Screaming tongues thrust out in alarm. Nothing beyond those tongues of pain. Misery was in his head. 'I am so miserable,' said the voice. He let the chant continue louder.

He must tell someone. He threw back his head and breathed hard. Holding the clean lamb, quiet in his hands, ears like lilies, he felt calmer. In the evening he went to the job that was his only employment, clear headed.

The note he was waiting for fell into the till between fivers. He pushed it in his pocket with his free hand as he handed the man some change. He looked him in the eye and gave him his simplest smile. Any letter was bad news for him. In the past he had hidden them or thrown them away. This one was expected. His heart beat in his throat as the white paper fluttered from the bank notes, but he was more confident now. But the words told him nothing. He had expected instructions, he anticipated a mission in the dark. 'Interested,' it said 'to see him.' No time, no place. It puzzled him. He remembered the last time and the last place and his insecurity returned. He saw his friend, the policeman, was unable to contact Lynne and wrote her a letter, presenting another difficulty. If he put letters in certain post boxes much before collection time, slugs would destroy them. It was too complicated to consider. In an anxiety attack, he tore the letter into small pieces.

He could not forget but could never act upon the idea of returning the money. It was too late now. He had agreed to inform the police if he walked into the remoter range of mountains. In times past he had started to build a wall from the ruined hill shack running down to firmer ground and a rutted road. Cautious now, he approached it from the lower end. It was restful, constructing, stone on stone, fitting the shapes together. He was still out of sight but at a point where the town and The Bell tower of the church were visible. This in particular gave him faith. He smoked a forbidden cigarette.

Away from walkers and picnic parties, notices had appeared in quite deserted places, nailed on posts to warn travellers away, and to keep to the footpath. With these notices there were others advertising meetings and property developments with land for sale. He disliked intrusion into his quiet places. So far it was rare to find strangers on a drovers route, hidden by woods of mixed hedge and pads of coarse grass. He wondered if his name was ever mentioned in the village but kept away. Night safely covered his movements and the hours of darkness were his favourite time.

Police ringed the hill. At nine o'clock he embarked on a form of Russian roulette. In his pocket a weapon. He had intended to ask for the return of the money but in the end his courage failed him. Instead he withdrew all his savings from the bank, an inadequate sum but naively he thought it might fool them. Failing light and cloud was a shield. He chose a route where the path crossed a waterfall, which in fine weather dried or trickled intermittently, walked beside the stone wall he had so carefully laid, and as the familiar chimney stack of his hideout came in sight, he paused to look westwards, for a moment forgetting why he had come. Light gleamed. It was his habit to count the last seconds of the sinking sun. Stopping he had lost his resolve. He turned and fell. As he got up his legs shook.

    He arrived too soon, too precipitately at the hut to consider exactly what he should do. Three paces away was a table, in the corner some slates. The packet with a message was a live thing in his hand. He gripped it hard and threw it at the black hole. He did not hear it land but saw it vanish through the door space. Deaf with fear he rolled himself over. Nothing moved in the long grasses, not a sound of wind in his ears as he sat up feeling his heartbeat. No one came. He considered going home but instead he crept below the wall to where it joined the back of the building. He could sense, he could feel it was occupied. He picked up a slate. He could only risk it once but it was a chance he would take. With great resolve he bowled it far down the wall. It cracked on stone. As if in answer to a bell, two men came out, stood motionless on the turf. He went to creep further on up the hill but at that moment they turned in his direction. An expanse of open ground stretched out in lighter and darker shadows. Had they guns? He experienced panic, but they turned back and climbed the wall further down where it was low and disappeared as the ground fell away. Had he fooled them? A tree bent by the wind spread across the yard and barn roof. Feet returning crushed stones and sticks. He heard conversation. He had fooled them once. They seemed to be progressing from the wall up the hill. He pulled himself onto a low branch. They turned. It was only the rustle of leaves or a bird's flight but they were coming back. He could not tell if he was high enough. They would see him if they pointed the torch that swung at their sides across to the tree. In the hut they crashed about. He put one hand on the roof and hung like a bat. When the cold made him stiff he let the roof take his weight. He tried to cover the sound with their movements but a slate split. It was just a crack but there was a silence below. Silence and someone listening. He remained poised, bent the way he had landed. He would wait. Without moving he tried to relax. Nothing seemed to happen. They could be asleep. Night birds called in the distance. He was ice cold. He must run for it. If he stayed till dawn he was trapped. Even now he feared his muscles would not respond as he eased himself to a standing position.

He breathed a prayer, jumped and ran, his knees buckled, his body shaking. He could hear no sound but his own footfalls thumping clumsily down the hill. He knew the way by shadows and the slope of the ground but he was at a disadvantage below them. He thought he heard voices. Then nothing. He had imagined voices but there was someone behind him. Lower and darker he hurled himself through bushes to a dried waterfall. He slid. The ragged edge of rock tore his legs. He was half-falling, saved only by the stone shelves angled on three sides. He held on to roots as he slid, hoping to catch the paths that the sheep made. Smaller rocks cascaded down. The sound must have given him away.

A road cut in the bank formed a horseshoe where, at the curve, any water sunk in a well was carried away by a pipe for several feet underground to fall into a ravine. As boys they had crawled through to peer down the precipice. From the top a torch flashed. He stepped in shadow. They would see him on the road. The torch went out. Not risking the rocks they were going round, he had time. An iron support stretched over the cliff, a foot away from the hard surface. A man desperate enough could hang on it and swing his legs into the drain. He acted. As it took his weight he arched his back and vanished like a snake into the dark hole. They were overhead, searching the trees to the right. Then steps to the left, one man above him, silence again. There was a sound of bushes parting, the pipe's length away, and a moment later, torchlight an inch or two from his face. The man above him was looking down the rock face thirty feet into a pit. All they would have to do was to kneel, bend down to look in to find him. Torchlight played on the small trees that grew in a fringe. Again it was gone. Footsteps indicated someone at the cliff edge. He heard slipping feet, a weight with a sound something like a sigh. Someone had fallen. He lay listening. What had silenced the owls? He was an animal trapped. In bad weather he could not have survived. Rushing water would have given him away and the numbing pain. His legs hurt, and the side of his face. He listened again for the voice. A second man was waiting somewhere out there. Instead he heard a motor. Shocked he saw the torch. He prayed and wished his life had been different. If he had his time again he would have done things better – different, better, all those things. Tears came into his eyes. As the torch shone full in his face he checked the noise deep in his throat, breathed in, stiffened each muscle from his face, arms and chest to his cold legs and stared into the beam. He was not afraid any more now it had come, this death, a blow, a shot perhaps. The pain had been hard and now, with no more cares, he turned his eyes to the orange light, unfocussed.

'It's all right!' said the shepherd.

'He felt weak,' he said, but with help got out, the fear of falling bringing him back to life. As they moved away cars, lights and men filled the hill.

'I don't know what you'd do without me.'

Men were investigating the alley. 'I always do the wrong thing,' Aledd said. Dr Lewis patched him up.

'Did she just drown?' He thought of the girl. For the first time he was able to think back. His memory must have some things wrong. There seemed to be someone else living his life.

'Lots of lovely stitches.'
'Was it so deep?'
'Long but not deep.'
'The waters are deep?'
'Pull yourself together, boy.' And he stuck the suture in.
'I want to know.'

'We don't know. Some things we'll never know.' He knew he must have done it wrong again but didn't say. 'Don't go judging. We're too fond of judging.'

'I'm glad we're leaving. I'm sorry, Edward, if you were happy here.' Numbed by what had happened, shock and sadness had kept Sylvia Bailey at home.

'My dear, it's better to start again.' But he had withdrawn safe inside his carapace with a daughter.

'Start? I'll never start anything again.' And later. 'I didn't know she was so unhappy.' The effort of raising her voice brought tears. 'Why didn't someone tell me? What was she doing, wandering on the mountain alone?'

'Don't think of it again. It may have been an accident. We must wait for the courts. The man you are thinking of was back at work. She was alone. I expect she fell. I'm going to pour you a drink.'

'I must keep the shop open for the season.'

'Very sensible.'

'That's all I can do.' She closed her eyes as the whisky burned down. 'A manager – a manageress.' She spoke in a sleep.

'Rosemary and Vanessa?'

'Rosemary's leaving.'

'Is she?'

'If one person leaves, they all leave. It happens. It unsettles the community. Quite contented people, happy with their houses, up and go when too many are leaving.'

'I didn't know too many were leaving.' Some answers he made through habit.

'We're leaving, that's enough.'

'Oh.'

'The Jeromes are never here. Gerald has a moving career. They're sending the vicar to Dorset.'

'I see what you mean.'

When they first filled in the Mawn Pool, Aledd did not speak of it.

'Never mind!' they said, guessing.

'Never mind, soon fill with water again. Peat!'

One day he and the shepherd went up together. Strangely, there was water, coming as if from underneath.

'Didn't make a very good job of it!'

Blackened and mud locked. The wheels of tractors marked the passage of machinery, and people had trodden new paths. The high plateau of the hill was lifeless as if nothing had ever happened there. He was trying to remember, and couldn't. Perhaps whatever had taken place had been wiped away.

'Look!' said his companion, 'the water's back. I told you.'

Aledd knew some things would not come back. 'Nothing comes back,' he said.

They returned the next day and the next. It was the best part of the summer. Water oozing, forming a pool, in the centre, the pile of debris, sinking. He could almost detect the moment when new ground emerged and shaped the contours of the water basin. When he was alone he would often hear the thump of an engine close by and would look down to see his shepherd friend below. He had taken to minding him, he supposed, like the sheep.

In the days that followed, tractors were ploughing his world up. The alley was full of people and machinery, mounting the slopes in a wave that came nearer. They ploughed hedges and bracken flat to his wall. A helicopter flapped over, disturbing the air. The group coming towards him moved aside to let a digger pass. He climbed higher. They moved inexorably to the place that had been his hideout and tore through it like paper. They crushed it to the last remnant of stone and went slowly back leaving behind a pile of dust in the heather.

The wind was light that summer. When the alien things had gone, life came back to him with the large birds. Kites circled and sheep appeared like flowers. The sun shone in each step he took back to the town. 'I'm happy now,' cried the song in his head, 'I am so happy,' it sobbed through him. A miracle. Something had happened to wash out all troubles, offences and wrongs done. The air was warm like cotton wool as evening came. There were still a few people. The shadows were long and peaceful and the weight behind his eyes lifted. He walked down the street in the old way, recognised himself, Aledd Vaughan.

He found work again at the refurbished Black Ox. Relaxed, he leant on the bar counter and looked idly through the long windows. Drunken Fred lurched in and took his drink to a corner table. Once seated, his morning pallor soon would change from grey to crimson. Aledd looked across to the high fields. Sheep were on the run, a dog, or feeding time. He could build another wall in the sun, more walls on the plain. He loved the stones that marked the landscape. Fred was watching him, coal black eyes gleaming in the dark.

'Have a drink!' An unprecedented offer, he had to say 'yes'.

The beer tasted bitter but at the same time unexpectedly sweet. He remembered he didn't like it but today was different and he would do different things.

The familiar figure of a woman stepped from a car and walked across the stretch of tarmac firmly on expensive heels. She entered and without buying a drink spoke to him like an old friend. His past employer looked altered, older, he thought and realised he had never seen her before at such close quarters. The angles and planes of her face were accentuated by shadows.

'Losing a daughter,' she said, 'the little shop needs you.'

'Fat chance!' said one from the corner.

And the other smiled, as the scar on his cheek burned.

'Please, Aledd.' It was always 'please' or 'why not'.

'I'm no good for you.'

She started to cry.

'See what I mean?' He put a hand on her shoulder and combed her hair back with his fingers as he used to.

'Silly,' he said as she sobbed in short, sharp breaths. 'Find someone...'

She knocked his hand away.

'I always do this to you. I don't want to.'

'We could have had one of the houses. Given it a name. Rent, it would really be ours. I was looking forward to it. I thought you were. I thought that was the idea.'

A word from the departing vicar had been his consolation and objective. He left the stones on the hill for a new land as he saw it.

After the communal purchase of Sylvia's shop, a decision to turn it into affordable accommodation for local people was considered to be inspired and given a final blessing from the Rev. Ben Tooley. It had produced instant action.

'After all,' he had said to Aledd, 'you were lucky to escape a summons or at least a reprimand. Community service would have been good for you. As it is, what could be better, new work, a stonemason, a chance to improve your skills.'

'I love stones,' he had said for the third time.

'The cottages are stone.'

'One is brick,' Aledd corrected.

'Of course. I remember, you worked there.'

'I don't understand you. Why?'

She is still a child, he thought, and I am older now, old in two years. 'Someone your own age,' he said.

'You're cruel!'

'Why? I want what's best for you.'

'That's the cruellest thing you could say. Find someone else is cruel.' She choked on the words in the way she always did. 'What have I done?'

'No, it's me. I don't think I'm right for it – marriage.' He brought himself to say the word.

'Dad says you're queer. It's that shepherd man, Mel. You're just a pimp.'

He had never seen her so angry. 'Mel?' He nearly laughed.

'He's an animal. Gross. Ugh,' she spat the words like a cat.

'Is that what you think?' He was stunned. Silence stood between them. In the silence she seemed to breathe more easily. Tears and words ended. He was emptied of emotion. Her outburst had overturned any idea he had had of her or himself.

'Mel!' he said again.

'And you're laughing,' she screamed, her fists in his face. They seemed to struggle for seconds and stood apart at last estranged.

'I'm not gay, you know,' he said seriously, 'but if I were, would it bother you?'

'Bother? You disgust me.'

'I'm sorry,' he said finally, 'if you wanted a proposal of

marriage this is not going to get you one.'

Tears filled her eyes again. She shook them down her cheeks where they hung on her chin. She stood stiffly and made no sound. Childish and vulnerable, he thought. He fumbled for something that might pass as a handkerchief and found a tissue creased with oil.

'Don't come near me. I suppose I always knew it. That's what it was.' She said the last words as if to herself.

'Darling.' He sounded old-fashioned, the word coming now as a farewell. It was not something he had ever contemplated. 'It's not true,' and later, 'I'm sorry, if that's what they're saying, I suppose I should feel insulted. Some are, but I'm not. I'm just a loner. I like beautiful things. I'm not an artist. I can't do anything well enough. I'd like to be. Or a craftsman. Listen now, listen.'

This speech made her turn away.

'I'm not gay. Sorry to disappoint you all.'

The notion that this could be his next public criticism hardly mattered now.

'What do you want of me?' he said at last.

'I don't know,' she said, 'I hoped we could go on.'

'Very well,' he said, 'what's wrong with that?' He touched her.

A village had grown in the flat land. The waters produced pastures of rich green. Sheep roamed the streets and the wild horses came down from the hills, leaving the safety of their secret places. One day, no one remembers when, the man vanished. No one saw him go. His work took him away and the familiar figure crossing the road or the plain had become less frequent. His disappearance was thought to be a bowing out.

'How sad!' they said. 'He built a village but couldn't live in it.'

The girl now had a fine house facing west, where the hills folded back to mountains and clouds. With four children, married to an airline pilot, they were a happy family. She had grown more beautiful with the years, used to being stared at, but had become less of a curiosity. It was the man who was missed, being a popular figure.

'Doesn't it seem strange?' someone asked her.

'No,' she replied.

The community grew closer. Certain similarities appeared again, contours in a face. Someone half recognised.

'Look, that's...' and people checked themselves calling out a name they should not mention. However, they were sure he was the man they had seen walking the wall out there on the hill, and he was still like a presence in the village of Maesford, as it was locally known, 'the town' being the other place despite documentation to the contrary. And his was the atmosphere of excitement, or lazy calm of a day, caught in a smile or some tools left idle.

'Will he come back?' they asked her.

'I don't know.'

'He never made you happy.'

'We had something wonderful.'

'He made you cry!'

'Yes,' she said.

'He could never make a woman happy.' And they would press her further. 'You are happy now?'

'Yes,' she said.

She made it a condition of marriage that she should remain in the district. 'We are born to live here,' she would say. 'It is part of us.'

Having married the most beautiful girl in the country, her husband was content to let her keep the gloomy mountains that looked picturesque in the summer.

The place was becoming more popular. Walkers were still requested to keep to the paths, and the area around the pool fenced off, together with the ravine and several stone buildings. There were so many stories; it was hard to believe they were true.

On warm evenings, Lynne could be seen, relaxed in her favourite seat, her hair shining in the dusk as the red sun dipped and sank. On other nights when the mist was back, she would pace up and down, her children playing round her feet. She kept to herself, kept the same habits and clothes; little had altered in her routine. There were subtle changes. Silk replaced the denim shirts, and her shoes were not bought in the market. Those who knew saw a badge of affluence in the buckles and labels and a small gold watch.

A gardener and a girl were employed, infrequently but enough to allow the lady of the house some hours of leisure. If callers were discouraged there was always stimulation at the moment of dismissal, or curiosity for those with whom contact was allowed.

On these occasions, a conversation might take place in the garden or furnished entrance hall. Doors leading to the downstairs rooms and, from a staircase, to those on the landing above, were kept tantalisingly shut.

Here a caller sat with Lynne for a time, the children as usual playing on the tiled floor, scattering bricks. 'I expect they're waiting for their daddy to come home.' Her latest visitor was persistent.

The mother laughed. It was like the sound of silver coins. The friend had reason to pause, unsure of what to say next. These people were so charged, the laugh, her curling hair, their wilful happiness. The laughter broke all contact. Nothing more was said.

As she left, the children hung on the gate and rode it to the ground. The day grew cool. She had reached the safe uniformity of the town before she found a measure of comfort.

Printed in the United Kingdom
by Lightning Source UK Ltd.
2458